The Last Egyptian

The Last Egyptian

L. Frank Baum

The Last Egyptian was first published in 1908.

This edition published by Mint Editions 2021.

ISBN 9781513211756 | E-ISBN 9781513210551

Published by Mint Editions®

MINT
EDITIONS

minteditionbooks.com

Publishing Director: Jennifer Newens
Design & Production: Rachel Lopez Metzger
Project Manager: Micaela Clark
Typesetting: Westchester Publishing Services

Contents

I

Where the Desert Meets the Nile

The sun fell hot upon the bosom of the Nile and clung there, vibrant, hesitating, yet aggressive, as if baffled in its desire to penetrate beneath the river's lurid surface. For the Nile defies the sun, and relegates him to his own broad domain, wherein his power is undisputed.

On either side the broad stream humanity shrank from Ra's seething disc. The shaduf workers had abandoned their skin-covered buckets and bamboo poles to seek shelter from the heat beneath a straggling tree or a straw mat elevated on stalks of ripe sugar-cane. The boats of the fishermen lay in little coves, where the sails were spread as awnings to shade their crews. The fellaheen laborers had all retired to their clay huts to sleep through this fiercest period of the afternoon heat.

On the Nile, however, a small steam dahabeah puffed lazily along, stemming with its slow motion the sweep of the mighty river toward the sea. The Arab stoker, naked and sweating, stood as far as possible from the little boiler and watched it with a look of absolute repulsion upon his swarthy face. The engineer, also an Arab, lay stretched upon the deck half asleep, but with both ears alert to catch any sound that might denote the fact that the straining, rickety engine was failing to perform its full duty. Back of the tiny cabin sat the dusky steersman, as naked and inert as his fellows, while under the deck awning reclined the one white man of the party, a young Englishman clothed in khaki knickerbockers and a white silk shirt well open at the throat.

There were no tourists in Egypt at this season. If you find a white man on the Nile in April, he is either attached to some exploration party engaged in excavations or a government employee from Cairo, Assyut or Luxor, bent upon an urgent mission.

The dahabeah was not a government boat, though, so that our Englishman was more likely to be an explorer than an official. It was evident he was no stranger to tropical climes, if we judged by his sun-browned skin and the quiet resignation to existing conditions with which he puffed his black briar and relaxed his muscular frame. He did not sleep, but lay with his head upon a low wicker rest that enabled him to sweep the banks of the Nile with his keen blue eyes.

The three Arabs regarded their master from time to time with stealthy glances, in which wonder was mingled with a certain respect. The foreigner was a fool to travel during the heat of the day; no doubt of that at all. The native knows when to work and when to sleep—a lesson the European never learns. Yet this was no casual adventurer exploiting his folly, but a man who had lived among them for years, who spoke Arabic fluently and could even cipher those hieroglyphics of the dead ages which abound throughout modern Egypt. Hassan, Abdallah and Ali knew this well, for they had accompanied Winston Bey on former expeditions, and heard him translate the ugly signs graven upon the ugly stones into excellent Arabic. It was all very wonderful in its way, but quite useless and impractical, if their opinion were allowed. And the master himself was impractical. He did foolish things at all times, and sacrificed his own comfort and that of his servants in order to accomplish unnecessary objects. Had he not paid well for his whims, Winston Bey might have sought followers in vain; but the Arab will even roast himself upon the Nile on an April afternoon to obtain the much-coveted gold of the European.

At four o'clock a slight breeze arose; but what matter? The journey was nearly done now. They had rounded a curve in the river, and ahead of them, lying close to the east bank, were the low mountains of Gebel Abu Fedah. At the south, where the rocks ended abruptly, lay a small grove of palms. Between the palms and the mountains was the beaten path leading from the Nile to the village of Al-Kusiyeh, a mile or so inland, which was the particular place the master had come so far and so fast to visit.

The breeze, although hardly felt, served to refresh the enervated travelers. Winston sat up and knocked the ashes from his pipe, making a careful scrutiny at the same time of the lifeless landscape ahead.

The mountains of gray limestone looked very uninviting as they lay reeking under the terrible heat of the sun. From their base to the river was no sign of vegetation, but only a hardened clay surface. The desert sands had drifted in in places. Even under the palms it lay in heavy drifts, for the land between the Nile and Al-Kusiyeh was abandoned to nature, and the fellaheen had never cared to redeem it.

The water was deep by the east bank, for the curve of the river swept the current close to the shore. The little dahabeah puffed noisily up to the bank and deposited the Englishman upon the hard clay. Then it backed across into shallow water, and Hassan shut down the engine while Abdallah dropped the anchor.

Winston now wore his cork helmet and carried a brown umbrella lined with green. With all his energy, the transition from the deck of the dahabeah to this oven-like atmosphere of the shore bade fair to overcome his resolution to proceed to the village.

But it would never do to recall his men so soon. They would consider it an acknowledgment that he had erred in judgment, and the only way to manage an Arab is to make him believe you know what you are about. The palm trees were not far away. He would rest in their shade until the sun was lower.

A dozen steps and the perspiration started from every pore. But he kept on, doggedly, until he came to the oblong shadow cast by the first palm, and there he squatted in the sand and mopped his face with his handkerchief.

The silence was oppressive. There was no sound of any kind to relieve it. Even the beetles were hidden far under the sand, and there was no habitation near enough for a donkey's bray or a camel's harsh growl to be heard. The Nile flows quietly at this point, and the boat had ceased to puff and rattle its machinery.

Winston brushed aside the top layer of sand with his hands, for that upon the surface was so hot that contact with it was unbearable. Then he extended his body to rest, turning slightly this way and that to catch in his face the faint breath of the breeze that passed between the mountains and the Nile. At the best he was doomed to an uncomfortable hour or two, and he cast longing glances at the other bits of shade to note whether any seemed more inviting than the one he had selected.

During this inspection his eye caught a patch of white some distance away. It was directly over the shadow of the furthest tree of the group, and aroused his curiosity. After a minute he arose in a leisurely fashion and walked over to the spot of white, which on nearer approach proved to be a soiled cotton tunic or burnous. It lay half buried in the sand, and at one end were the folds of a dirty turban, with faded red and yellow stripes running across the coarse cloth.

Winston put his foot on the burnous and the thing stirred and emitted a muffled growl. At that he kicked the form viciously; but now it neither stirred nor made a sound. Instead, a narrow slit appeared between the folds of the turban, and an eye, black and glistening, looked steadfastly upon the intruder.

"Do you take me for a beast, you imbecile, that you dare to disturb my slumbers?" asked a calm voice, in Arabic.

The heat had made Winston Bey impatient.

"Yes; you are a dog. Get up!" he commanded, kicking the form again.

The turban was removed, disclosing a face, and the man sat up, crossing his bare legs beneath him as he stared fixedly at his persecutor.

Aside from the coarse burnous, sadly discolored in many places, the fellow was unclothed. His skin showed at the breast and below his knees, and did not convey an impression of immaculate cleanliness. Of slender build, with broad shoulders, long hands and feet and sinewy arms and legs, the form disclosed was curiously like those so often presented in the picture-writing upon the walls of ancient temples. His forehead was high, his chin square, his eyes large and soft, his cheeks full, his mouth wide and sensual, his nose short and rounded. His jaws protruded slightly and his hair was smooth and fine. In color the tint of his skin was not darker than the tanned cuticle of the Englishman, but the brown was softer, and resembled coffee that has been plentifully diluted with cream. A handsome fellow in his way, with an expression rather unconcerned than dignified, which masked a countenance calculated to baffle even a shrewder and more experienced observer than Winston Bey.

Said the Englishman, looking at him closely:

"You are a Copt."

Inadvertently he had spoken in his mother tongue and the man laughed.

"If you follow the common prejudice and consider every Copt a Christian," he returned in purest English, "then I am no Copt; but if you mean that I am an Egyptian, and no dog of an Arab, then, indeed, you are correct in your estimate."

Winston uttered an involuntary exclamation of surprise. For a native to speak English is not so unusual; but none that he knew expressed himself with the same ease and confidence indicated in this man's reply. He brushed away some of the superheated sand and sat down facing his new acquaintance.

"Perhaps," said he—a touch of sarcasm in his voice—"I am speaking with a descendant of the Great Rameses himself."

"Better than that," rejoined the other, coolly. "My forefather was Ahtka-Rā, of true royal blood, who ruled the second Rameses as cleverly as that foolish monarch imagined he ruled the Egyptians."

Winston seemed amused.

"I regret," said he, with mock politeness, "that I have never before heard of your great forefather."

"But why should you?" asked the Egyptian. "You are, I suppose, one of those uneasy investigators that prowl through Egypt in a stupid endeavor to decipher the inscriptions on the old temples and tombs. You can read a little—yes; but that little puzzles and confuses you. Your most learned scholars—your Mariettes and Petries and Masperos—discover one clue and guess at twenty, and so build up a wonderful history of the ancient kings that is absurd to those who know the true records."

"Who knows them?" asked Winston, quickly.

The man dropped his eyes.

"No one, perhaps," he mumbled. "At the best, but one or two. But you would know more if you first studied the language of the ancient Egyptians, so that when you deciphered the signs and picture writings you could tell with some degree of certainty what they meant."

Winston sniffed. "Answer my question!" said he, sternly. "Who knows the true records, and where are they?"

"Ah, I am very ignorant," said the other, shaking his head with an humble expression. "Who am I, the poor Kāra, to dispute with the scholars of Europe?"

The Englishman fanned himself with his helmet and sat silent for a time.

"But this ancestor of yours—the man who ruled the Great Rameses—who was he?" he asked, presently.

"Men called him Ahtka-Rā, as I said. He was descended from the famous Queen Hatshepset, and his blood was pure. Indeed, my ancestor should have ruled Egypt as its king, had not the first Rameses overthrown the line of Mēnēs and established a dynasty of his own. But Ahtka-Rā, unable to rule in his own name, nevertheless ruled through the weak Rameses, under whom he bore the titles of High Priest of Āmen, Lord of the Harvests and Chief Treasurer. All of the kingdom he controlled and managed, sending Rameses to wars to keep him occupied, and then, when the king returned, setting him to build temples and palaces, and to erect monuments to himself, that he might have no excuse to interfere with the real business of the government. You, therefore, who read the inscriptions of the vain king wonder at his power and call him great; and, in your ignorance, you know not even the name of Ahtka-Rā, the most wonderful ruler that Egypt has ever known."

"It is true that we do not know him," returned Winston, scrutinizing the man before him with a puzzled expression. "You seem better informed than the Egyptologists!"

Kāra dipped his hands into the sand beside him and let the grains slip between his fingers, watching them thoughtfully.

"Rameses the Second," said he, "reigned sixty-five years, and—"

"Sixty-seven years," corrected Winston. "It is written."

"In the inscriptions, which are false," explained the Egyptian. "My ancestor concealed the death of Rameses for two years, because Meremptah, who would succeed him, was a deadly enemy. But Meremptah discovered the secret at last, and at once killed Ahtka-Rā, who was very old and unable to oppose him longer. And after that the treasure cities of Pithom and Raamses, which my ancestor had built, were seized by the new king, but no treasures were found in them. Even in death my great ancestor was able to deceive and humble his enemies."

"Listen, Kāra," said Winston, his voice trembling with suppressed eagerness; "to know that which you have told to me means that you have discovered some sort of record hitherto unknown to scientists. To us who are striving to unravel the mystery of ancient Egyptian history this information will be invaluable. Let me share your knowledge, and tell me what you require in exchange for your secret. You are poor; I will make you rich. You are unknown; I will make the name of Kāra famous. You are young; you shall enjoy life. Speak, my brother, and believe that I will deal justly by you—on the word of an Englishman."

The Egyptian did not even look up, but continued playing with the sand. Yet over his grave features a smile slowly spread.

"It is not five minutes," he murmured softly, "since I was twice kicked and called a dog. Now I am the Englishman's brother, and he will make me rich and famous."

Winston frowned, as if he would like to kick the fellow again. But he resisted the temptation.

"What would you?" he asked, indifferently. "The burnous might mean an Arab. It is good for the Arab to be kicked at times."

Possibly Kāra neither saw the jest nor understood the apology. His unreadable countenance was still turned toward the sand, and he answered nothing.

The Englishman moved uneasily. Then he extracted a cigarette case from his pocket, opened it, and extended it toward the Egyptian.

Kāra looked at the cigarettes and his face bore the first expression of interest it had yet shown. Very deliberately he bowed, touched his forehead and then his heart with his right hand, and afterward leaned forward and calmly selected a cigarette.

Winston produced a match and lighted it, the Egyptian's eyes seriously following his every motion. He applied the light to his own cigarette first; then to that of Kāra. Another touch of the forehead and breast and the native was luxuriously inhaling the smoke of the tobacco. His eyes were brighter and he wore a look of great content.

The Englishman silently watched until the other had taken his third whiff; then, the ceremonial being completed, he spoke, choosing his words carefully.

"Seek as we may, my brother, for the records of the dead civilization of your native land, we know full well that the most important documents will be discovered in the future, as in the past, by the modern Egyptians themselves. Your traditions, handed down through many generations, give to you a secret knowledge of where the important papyri and tablets are deposited. If there are hidden tombs in Gebel Abu Fedah, or near the city of Al-Kusiyeh, perhaps you know where to find them; and if so, we will open them together and profit equally by what we secure."

The Egyptian shook his head and flicked the ash from his cigarette with an annoyed gesture.

"You are wrong in estimating the source of my knowledge," said he, in a tone that was slightly acrimonious. "Look at my rags," spreading his arms outward; "would I refuse your bribe if I knew how to earn it? I have not smoked a cigarette before in months—not since Tadros the dragoman came to Al Fedah in the winter. I am barefoot, because I fear to wear out my sandals until I know how to replace them. Often I am hungry, and I live like a jackal, shrinking from all intercourse with my fellows or with the world. That is Kāra, the son of kings, the royal one!"

Winston was astonished. It is seldom a native complains of his lot or resents his condition, however lowly it may be. Yet here was one absolutely rebellious.

"Why?" he asked.

"Because my high birth isolates me," was the reply, with an accent of pride. "It is no comfortable thing to be Kāra, the lineal descendant of the great Ahtka-Rā, in the days when Egypt's power is gone, and her children are scorned by the Arab Muslims and buffeted by the English Christians."

"Do you live in the village?" asked Winston.

"No; my burrow is in a huddle of huts behind the mountain, in a place that is called Fedah."

"With whom do you live?"

"My grandmother, Hatatcha."

"Ah!"

"You have heard of her?"

"No; I was thinking only of an Egyptian Princess Hatatcha who set fashionable London crazy in my father's time."

Kāra leaned forward eagerly, and then cast a half fearful glance around, at the mountains, the desert, and the Nile.

"Tell me about her!" he said, sinking his voice to a whisper.

"About the Princess?" asked Winston, surprised. "Really, I know little of her history. She came in a flash of wonderful oriental magnificence, I have heard, and soon had the nobility of England suing for her favors. Lord Roane especially divorced his wife that he might marry the beautiful Egyptian; and then she refused to wed with him. There were scandals in plenty before Hatatcha disappeared from London, which she did as mysteriously as she had come, and without a day's warning. I remember that certain infatuated admirers spent fortunes in search of her, overrunning all Egypt, but without avail. No one has ever heard of her since."

Kāra drew a deep breath, sighing softly.

"It was like my grandmother," he murmured. "She was always a daughter of Set."

Winston stared at him.

"Do you mean to say—" he began.

"Yes," whispered Kāra, casting another frightened look around; "it was my grandmother, Hatatcha, who did that. You must not tell, my brother, for she is still in league with the devils and would destroy us both if she came to hate us. Her daughter, who was my mother, was the child of that same Lord Roane you have mentioned; but she never knew her father nor England. I myself have never been a day's journey from the Nile, for Hatatcha makes me her slave."

"She must be very old, if she still lives," said Winston, musingly.

"She was seventeen when she went to London," replied Kāra, "and she returned here in three years, with my mother in her arms. Her daughter was thirty-five when I was born, and that is twenty-three years ago. Fifty-eight is not an advanced age, yet Hatatcha was a withered hag when first I remember her, and she is the same today.

By the head of Osiris, my brother, she is likely to live until I am stiff in my tomb."

"It was she who taught you to speak English?"

"Yes. I knew it when I was a baby, for in our private converse she has always used the English tongue. Also I speak the ancient Egyptian language, which you call the Coptic, and I read correctly the hieroglyphics and picture-writings of my ancestors. The Arabic, of course, I know. Hatatcha has been a careful teacher."

"What of your mother?" asked Winston.

"Why, she ran away when I was a child, to enter the harem of an Arab in Cairo, so that she passed out of our lives, and I have lived with my grandmother always."

"I am impressed by the fact," said the Englishman, with a sneer, "that your royal blood is not so pure after all."

"And why not?" returned Kāra, composedly. "Is it not from the mother we descend? Who my grandfather may have been matters little, provided Hatatcha, the royal one, is my granddame. Perhaps my mother never considered who my father might be; it was unimportant. From her I drew the blood of the great Ahtka-Rā, who lives again in me. Robbed of your hollow ceremonial of marriage, you people of Europe can boast no true descent save through your mothers—no purer blood than I, ignoring my fathers, am sure now courses in my veins; for the father, giving so little to his progeny, can scarcely contaminate it, whatever he may chance to be."

The other, paying little heed to this discourse, the platitudes of which were all too familiar to his ears, reflected deeply on the strange discovery he had made through this unconventional Egyptian.

"Then," said he, pursuing his train of thought, "your knowledge of your ancestry and the life and works of Ahtka-Rā was obtained through your grandmother?"

"Yes."

"And she has not disclosed to you how it is that she knows all this?"

"No. She says it is true, and I believe it. Hatatcha is a wonderful woman."

"I agree with you. Where did she get the money that enabled her to amaze all England with her magnificence and splendor?"

"I do not know."

"Is she wealthy now?"

Kāra laughed.

"Did I not say we were half starved, and live like foxes in a hole? For raiment we have each one ragged garment. But the outside of man matters little, save to those who have nothing within. Treasures may be kept in a rotten chest."

"But personally you would prefer a handsome casket?"

"Of course. It is Hatatcha who teaches me philosophy to make me forget my rags."

The Englishman reflected.

"Do you labor in the fields?" he asked.

"She will not let me," said Kāra. "If my wrongs were righted, she holds, I would even now be king of Egypt. The certainty that they will never be righted does not alter the morale of the case."

"Does Hatatcha earn money herself?"

"She sits in her hut morning and night, muttering curses upon her enemies."

"Then how do you live at all?"

Kāra seemed surprised by the question, and considered carefully his reply.

"At times," said he, "when our needs are greatest, my grandmother will produce an ancient coin of the reign of Hystaspes, which the sheik at Al-Kusiyeh readily changes into piasters, because they will give him a good premium on it at the museum in Cairo. Once, years ago, the sheik threatened Hatatcha unless she confessed where she had found these coins; but my grandmother called Set to her aid, and cast a spell upon the sheik, so that his camels died of rot and his children became blind. After that he let Hatatcha alone, but he was still glad to get her coins."

"Where does she keep them?"

"It is her secret. When she was ill, a month ago, and lay like one dead, I searched everywhere for treasure and found it not. Perhaps she has exhausted her store."

"Had she anything besides the coins?"

"Once a jewel, which she sent by Tadros, the dragoman, to exchange for English books in Cairo."

"What became of the books?"

"After we had both read them they disappeared. I do not know what became of them."

They had shifted their seats twice, because the shadow cast by the palms moved as the sun drew nearer to the horizon. Now the patches were long and narrow, and there was a cooler breath in the air.

The Englishman sat long silent, thinking intently. Kāra was placidly smoking his third cigarette.

The rivalry among excavators and Egyptologists generally is intense. All are eager to be recognized as discoverers. Since the lucky find of the plucky American, Davis, the explorers among the ancient ruins of Egypt had been on the qui vive to unearth some farther record of antiquity to startle and interest the scholars of the world. Much of value has been found along the Nile banks, it is true; but it is generally believed that much more remains to be discovered.

Gerald Winston, with a fortune at his command and a passion for Egyptology, was an indefatigable prospector in this fascinating field, and it was because of a rumor that ancient coins and jewels had come from the Sheik of Al-Kusiyeh that he had resolved to visit that village in person and endeavor to learn the secret source of this wealth before someone else forestalled him.

The story that he had just heard from the lips of the voluble Kāra rendered his visit to Al-Kusiyeh unnecessary; but that he was now on the trail of an important discovery was quite clear to him. How best to master the delicate conditions confronting him must be a subject of careful consideration, for any mistake on his part would ruin all his hopes.

"If my brother obtains any further valuable knowledge," said he, finally, "he will wish to sell it to good advantage. And it is evident to both of us that old Hatatcha has visited some secret tomb, from whence she has taken the treasure that enabled her to astound London for a brief period. When her wealth was exhausted she was forced to return to her squalid surroundings, and by dint of strict economy has lived upon the few coins that remained to her until now. Knowing part of your grandmother's story, it is easy to guess the remainder. The coins of Darius Hystaspes date about five hundred years before Christ, so that they would not account for Hatatcha's ample knowledge of a period two thousand years earlier. But mark me, Kāra, the tomb from which your grandmother extracted such treasure must of necessity contain much else—not such things as the old woman could dispose of without suspicion, but records and relics which in my hands would be invaluable, and for which I would gladly pay you thousands of piasters. See what you can do to aid me to bring about this desirable result. If you can manage to win the secret from your grandmother, you need be her slave no longer. You may go to Cairo and see the dancing girls and spend your money freely; or you can buy donkeys and a camel, and set up for a sheik. Meantime I will keep my dahabeah in this vicinity, and everyday I will pass this spot at sundown and await for you to signal me. Is it all clear to you, my brother?"

"It is as crystal," answered the Egyptian gravely.

He took another cigarette, lighted it with graceful composure, and rose to his feet. Winston also stood up.

The sun had dropped behind the far corner of Gebel Abu Fedah, and with the grateful shade the breeze had freshened and slightly cooled the tepid atmosphere.

Wrapping his burnous around his tall figure, Kāra made dignified obeisance.

"Osiris guard thee, my brother," said he.

"May Horus grant thee peace," answered Winston, humoring this disciple of the most ancient religion. Then he watched the Egyptian stalk proudly away over the hot sands, his figure erect, his step slow and methodical, his bearing absurdly dignified when contrasted with his dirty tunic and unwashed skin.

"I am in luck," he thought, turning toward the bank to summon Hassan and Abdallah; "for I have aroused the rascal's cupidity, and he will soon turn up something or other, I'll be bound. Ugh! the dirty beast."

At the foot of the mountains Kāra paused abruptly and stood motionless, staring moodily at the sands before him.

"It was worth the bother to get the cigarettes," he muttered. Then he added, with sudden fierceness: "Twice he spurned me with his foot, and called me 'dog'!"

And he spat in the sand and continued on his way.

II

Hatatcha

The mountains of Abu Fedah consist of a low range about twelve miles long and from two to three hundred feet in height. These hills are wedge-shaped, and from a narrow, uneven ridge at the summit the sides slope downward at a sharp angle on either side, affording little apparent foothold to one who might essay to climb the steeps. At the south end are pits wherein were found numbers of mummified crocodiles, proving that these reptiles were formerly worshipped by the natives of Al-Kusiyeh, which is the ancient city of Qes of the hieroglyphic texts, and was afterward called Cusae by the Greeks. It was, in its prime, the capital of the fourteenth nome or province of Upper Egypt, and a favorite winter abode of the kings of the Middle Empire. The modern village, as before explained, lies a mile or two from the Nile bank, in a fertile valley watered by bubbling springs. The inhabitants are mostly Arabs, or a mixture of the Arab blood with that of the native fellaheen, which last, in common with the Copts, are direct descendants of the ancient Egyptians.

The early Egyptologists expected to find important tombs secreted in the limestone cliffs of Gebel Abu Fedah; but careful search only revealed the mummy crocodile pits and a few scattering and uninteresting cavities roughly hewn in the rocks, which might have contained mummies at one time, but had been rifled of their contents ages ago. The few inscriptions remaining in these rock tombs indicated that they were the burial places of ordinary citizens of Qes, and such cavities as were observed all faced the Nile. The opposite slopes of the mountains, facing the east, seemed never to have been utilized for tombs, fond as the Egyptians were of such opportunities to inter their dead in rocky places, above the reach of jackals or marauders.

Kāra skirted the south end of the mountain and passed around the edge of a bleak gray cliff. Here, close against the overhanging sandstone, was clustered a nest of wretched hovels, built partially of loose fragments of rock and partly of Nile mud baked in the sun. The place was called Fedah by the natives, and its scant dozen of inhabitants were those of pure Egyptian lineage, who refused to mingle with the natives of Al-Kusiyeh.

The most substantial of the dwellings was that occupied by Hatatcha and her grandson. It had been built against a hollow or cave of the mountain, so that the cane roof projected only a few feet beyond the cliff. A rude attempt on the part of the builders to make the front wall symmetrical was indicated by the fact that the stones bore quarry marks, and at the entrance arch, which had never been supplied with a door, but was half concealed by a woven mat, the stones were fully four feet in thickness.

The other huts, ranged beside and before this one, were far less imposing in construction; but all had the appearance of great antiquity, and those at the north and south edges of the huddle were unoccupied and more or less ruined and neglected. Tradition said that Fedah, in spite of its modern Arabic name, was as old as ancient Qes, and there was no reason to doubt the statement. Its location was admirable in summer, for the mountain shaded it during the long hot afternoons; but around it was nothing but sand and rock, and the desert stretched in front as far as the borders of Al-Kusiyeh.

Kāra, entering the short and narrow street between the hovels, pushed a goat from his path and proceeded calmly toward his dwelling. As he entered its one room, he paused to allow his eyes to grow accustomed to the gloom and then gazed around with an expression of mild surprise.

In one corner, upon a bed of dried rushes, lay the form of an old woman. Her single black cotton garment was open at the throat, displaying a wrinkled, shrunken bosom that rose and fell spasmodically, as if the hag breathed with great effort. Her eyes were closed and the scant, tousled locks of fine gray hair surrounding her face gave it a weird and witch-like expression. In spite of her age and the clime in which she ad lived, Hatatcha's skin was almost as white as that of Europeans, its tint being so delicate as to be scarcely noticeable.

Upon a short wooden bench beside the rushes sat a girl with a palm branch, which she swayed back and forth to keep the flies from settling upon Hatatcha's face. She was, perhaps, fifteen years of age, but as fully matured in form as an English girl of twenty-five. Her face was remarkably handsome from the standpoint of regularity of contour, but its absolute lack of expression would render it uninviting to a connoisseur of beauty. Her dark eyes were magnificent, and seemed to have depths which were disappointing when you probed them. She wore the conventional black gown, or tunic, but because of the heat had allowed it to slip down to her waist, leaving her shoulders and breasts bare.

After a long and thoughtful look at his grandmother, Kāra sat down beside the girl and put his arm around her, drawing her close to his body. She neither resented the caress nor responded to it, but yielded herself inertly to the embrace while she continued to sway the palm branch with her free right arm.

"Ah, my Nephthys," said the man, lightly, in the Coptic tongue, "is our Hatatcha in the grip of the devils again?"

The girl made no reply, but at the sound of Kāra's voice the old woman opened her great eyes and gazed for an instant steadfastly upon her grandson. Her hands, which had been nervously clutching her robe, were raised in supplication, and she said in English, in a weak, hoarse voice:

"The draught, Kāra! Be quick!"

The man hesitated, but released the girl and stood up.

"It is the last, my Hatatcha. You know that no more can be procured," he said, in protest.

"I shall need no more," she answered, with much difficulty. "It is the last time. Be quick, Kāra!" Her voice died away in an odd gurgle, and her chest fluttered as if the breath was about to leave it.

Kāra, watching her curiously, as a dog might, was impressed by the symptoms. He turned to Nephthys.

"Go out," he commanded, in Coptic, and the girl arose and passed under the arch.

Then he went to a part of the wall and removed a loose stone, displaying a secret cavity. From this he took a small vase, smooth and black, which had a stopper of dull metal. Carrying it to Hatatcha, he knelt down, removed the stopper and placed the neck of the vase to her lips. The delicate, talon-like fingers clutched the vessel eagerly and the woman drank, while Kāra followed the course of the liquid down her gullet by watching her skinny throat.

When it was done, he carried the empty vase back to the crypt and replaced the loose stone. Then he returned to the bedside and sat down upon the bench. A bowl containing some bits of bread stood near. He stooped and caught a piece in his fingers, munching it between his strong teeth while he stared down upon Hatatcha's motionless form.

It was quite dark in the room by this time, for twilights are short in Egypt. But the pupils of the man's eyes expanded like those of a cat, and he could follow the slow rise and fall of the woman's chest and knew she was again breathing easily.

An hour passed, during which Kāra moved but once, to drink from a jar standing in the opposite corner. Hatatcha's condition disturbed him. If she died, he would be at a loss what to do. Unused to work and without resource of any sort, life would become a burden to him. He was, moreover, accustomed to be led by the strong old woman in all things, and she had been the provider during all the twenty-three years of his life. Kāra had been trained to think deeply upon many subjects, but here was one which had never occurred to him before because Hatatcha had never discussed it, and the matter of her death was until lately a thing that did not need to be considered. But her condition was serious tonight, and the precious life-giving elixir was gone to the last drop.

All the people around Abu Fedah deferred to Hatatcha, because she claimed, with some show of reason, to be of royal descent. But they did not know the story of Ahtka-Rā, and her escapades in London years ago were all unsuspected by them. Hatatcha only confided such things to Kāra, and he would never dare breathe them to any except the Englishman, from whose lips the tales would never be liable to return.

But there was a great deal that Kāra himself did not know, and he realized this as he gazed uneasily upon his sick grandparent. She ought to tell him where the coins and jewels had come from, and if there were any left. He would need some trifles of that sort when she was gone. And the matter of her funeral—she had expressed strange desires, at times, regarding the disposition of her body after death. How was he to find means to carry out such desires?

A voice, low and clear, fell upon his ear and made him start. Hatatcha's big eyes were open and he caught their sparkle even in the darkness.

"Come nearer," she said.

He dropped upon the floor at her side and sat cross-legged near her head, bending over to catch her slightest whisper. She spoke in English to him.

"Anubis calls me, my son, and I must join his kingdom. My years are not great, but they have worn out my body with love and hatreds and plans of vengeance. You are my successor, and the inheritor of my treasures and my revenge and hates. The time is come when you must repay my care and perform a mission for which I have trained you since childhood. Promise me that you will fulfil my every wish to the letter!"

"Of necessity, Hatatcha," he responded, calmly. "Are you not my grandmother?"

She remained silent a moment.

"You are cold, and selfish and cruel," she resumed, her tone hardening, "and I have made you so. You are intelligent, and fearless, and strong. It is due to my training. Listen, then! Once I was young and beautiful and loving, and when I faced the world it fell at my feet in adoration. But one who claimed to be a man crushed all the joy and love from my heart, and left me desolate and broken. Like a spurned hind, I crept from the glare of palaces back to my mud hut, bearing my child in my arms, and here I mourned and suffered for years and found no comfort. Then the love that had destroyed my peace fell away, and in its place Set planted the seeds of vengeance. These I have cherished, and lo! a tree has sprouted and grown, of which you, my son, are the stalwart trunk. The fruit has been long maturing, but it is now ripe. Presently you, too, will face the world; but as a man—not like the weak woman I was—and you will accomplish my revenge. Is it not so, my Kāra?"

"If you say it, my Hatatcha, it is so," he answered. But he wondered.

"Then pay close attention to my words," she continued, "and store them carefully in your mind, that nothing shall be forgotten when it is needed to assist you. I will explain all things while I have the strength of the elixir, for when it leaves me my breath will go with it, and then your labors will begin."

Kāra leaned still lower. For once his heart beat faster than was its custom, and he felt a thrill of excitement pervading his entire being. The climax in his life had at last arrived, and he was about to discover what things he was destined to accomplish in the great unknown world.

Hour after hour Hatatcha's low voice continued to instruct her grandson. Occasionally she would question him, to be sure that he understood, and several names she made him repeat many times, until they were indelibly impressed upon his memory.

At last she took the forefinger of his right hand and with it made a mystic sign upon her naked breast, making him repeat after her a dreadful oath to obey her instructions in every way and keep forever certain grave secrets.

Then she fell back and lay still.

Daybreak came in time, and a streak of light crept under the arch and touched the group in the corner.

The aged hag, filthy and unkempt, lay dead upon her couch of rushes, and beside her sat Kāra, his face immobile, his eyes staring fixedly at the opposite wall.

He was thinking.

III

The Dragoman

Nephthys came from her mother's hut in the cool of early morning, bearing on her head an earthen jar. She was bound for the river, to carry from thence their daily supply of water.

As she passed Hatatcha's dwelling she found Kāra standing in the archway, and he drew the girl toward him and kissed her lips. They were cold and unresponsive.

"How is your grandmother?" she asked, indifferently.

"She is with Isis," he answered, holding her arm with one hand and feeling her brown cheek with the other.

The girl shuddered and glanced askance at the arch.

"Let me go," she said.

Instead, he folded an arm around her and kissed her again, while she put up a hand to steady the jar from falling.

Then Kāra experienced a sudden surprise. His body spun around like a top and was hurled with force against the opposite wall. At the same time the jar toppled from Nephthys' head and was shattered on the ground. The girl staggered back and leaned against the stones of the arch, staring at the path ahead.

In front of her stood a young man most gorgeously arrayed. A red fez, such as many wear in Egypt, was perched jauntily upon his head. Covering his breast was a blue satin jacket elaborately braided with silver, and where it parted in front a vest of white silk showed, with a line of bright silver buttons. His knee breeches were of saffron pongee, wide and flowing, like those of a Turk, and from there down to his yellow slippers his legs were bare. Add a voluminous sash of crimson silk and a flowing mantle suspended from his shoulders, and you can guess the splendor of the man's attire.

His person was short and inclined to stoutness, and his face, with its carefully curled black mustache, was remarkably regular and handsome. His eyes were nearly as large and black as Kāra's, and at the present moment they flashed fire, while an angry frown distorted his brow. He stood with his legs spread apart and his hands pressed upon his hips, regarding the girl with a glance of sullen fury.

Nephthys returned the look with one of stupor. Her face was quite as expressionless as before, but her nostrils dilated a little, as if she were afraid.

"Tadros!" she muttered.

Kāra lifted his tall form from the ground and stood scowling upon his assailant.

"The cursed dragoman again!" he exclaimed, with bitterness.

Tadros turned his head slightly to direct a look of scorn upon his enemy. Then he regarded the girl again.

"What of your promise to me, woman?" he demanded, sternly. "Are you the plaything of every dirty Egyptian when my back is turned?"

Nephthys had no reply. She looked at the pattern of the silver braid upon his jacket and followed carefully its curves and twists. The blue satin was the color of lapis lazuli, she thought, and the costume must have cost a lot of money—perhaps as much as fifty piasters.

"Your mother shall answer for this perfidy," continued the dragoman, in Arabic. "If I am to be toyed with and befooled, I will have my betrothal money back—every piaster of it!"

The girl's eyes dropped to her feet and examined the fragments of the jar.

"It is broken!" she said, with a wailing accent.

"Bah! there are more at Keneh," he returned, kicking away a bit of the earthenware. "It will cost old Sĕra more than the jar if she does not rule you better. Come!"

He waved his hand pompously and strutted past her to the door of her mother's hut, paying no heed to the evil looks of Kāra, who still stood motionless in his place.

The girl followed, meek and obedient.

They entered a square room lighted by two holes in the mud walls. The furniture was rude and scanty, and the beds were rushes from the Nile. A black goat that had a white spot over its left eye stood ruminating with its head out of one of the holes.

A little withered woman with an erect form and a pleasant face met Tadros, the dragoman, just within the doorway.

"Welcome!" she said, crossing her arms upon her breast and bending her head until she was nearly double.

"Peace to this house," returned Tadros, carelessly, and threw himself upon a bench.

Sĕra squatted upon the earthen floor and looked with pride and satisfaction at the dragoman's costume.

"You are a great man, my Tadros," she said, "and you must be getting rich. We are honored by your splendid presence. Gaze upon your affianced bride, O Dragoman! Is she not getting fat and soft in flesh, and fit to grace your most select harem?"

"I must talk to you about Nephthys," said the dragoman, lighting a cigarette. "She is too free with these dirty Fedahs, and especially with that beast Kāra."

His tone had grown even and composed by this time, and his face had lost its look of anger.

"What would you have?" asked old Sĕra, deprecatingly. "The girl must carry water and help me with the work until you take her away with you. I cannot keep her secluded like a princess. And there are no men in Fedah except old Nikko, who is blind, and young Kāra, who is not."

"It is Kāra who annoys me," said Tadros, puffing his cigarette lazily.

"Kāra! But he is the royal one. You know that well enough. The descendant of the ancient kings has certain liberties, and therefore takes others, and he merely indulges in a kiss now and then. I have watched him, and it does not worry me."

"The royal one!" repeated the dragoman scornfully. "How do we know old Hatatcha's tales are true?"

"They must be true," returned Sĕra, positively. "My mother served Hatatcha's mother, because she was the daughter of kings. For generations the ancestors of Kāra have been revered by those who were Egyptians, although their throne is a dream of the past, and they are condemned to live in poverty. Be reasonable, my Tadros! Your own blood is as pure as ours, even though it is not royal. What! shall we Egyptians forget our dignity and rub skins with the English dogs or the pagan Arabs?"

"The Arabs are not so bad," said Tadros, thoughtfully. "They have many sensible customs, which we are bound to accept; for these Muslims overrun our country and are here to stay. Nor are the simple English to be sneered at, my Sĕra. I know them well, and also their allies, the Americans and the Germans and French. They travel far to see Cairo and our Nile, and drop golden sovereigns into my pockets because I guide them to the monuments and explain their history, and at the same time keep the clever Arabs from robbing them until after I am paid. Yes; all people have their uses, believe me."

"Ah, you are wonderful!" exclaimed the old woman, with earnest conviction.

"I am dragoman," returned the man, proudly, "and my name is known from Cairo to Khartoum." He tossed a cigarette at Sĕra, who caught it deftly and put it between her lips. Then he graciously allowed her to obtain a light from his own cigarette.

Meantime, Nephthys, on entering the hut behind Tadros, had walked to the further side of the room and lifted the lid of a rude chest, rough hewn from eucalyptus wood. From this she drew a bundle, afterward closing the lid and spreading the contents of the bundle upon the chest. Then she turned her back to the others, unfastened her dusty black gown, and allowed it to fall to her hips. Over her head she dropped a white tunic, and afterward a robe of coarse gauze covered thickly with cheap spangles. She now stepped out of the black gown and hung it upon a peg. A broad gilt belt was next clasped around her waist—loosely, so as not to confine too close the folds of spangled gauze.

Tadros, during his conversation with Sĕra, watched this transformation of his betrothed with satisfaction. When she had twined a vine of artificial flowers in her dark hair, the girl came to him and sat upon his knee. Her feet were still bare, and not very clean; but he did not notice that.

"I will speak to Hatatcha about Kāra," remarked the old woman, inhaling the smoke of her cigarette with evident enjoyment, "and she will tell him to be more careful."

"Hatatcha is dead," said Nephthys.

Sĕra stared a moment and dropped her cigarette. Then she uttered a shrill wail and threw her skirt over her head, swaying back and forth.

"Shut up!" cried the dragoman, jerking away the cloth. "It is time enough to wail when the mourners assemble."

Sĕra picked up her cigarette.

"When did Hatatcha go to Anubis?" she asked her daughter.

"Kāra did not say," returned the girl. "I was with her at the last sunset, and she was dying then."

"It matters nothing," said the dragoman, carelessly. "Hatatcha is better off in the nether world, and her rascally grandson must now go to work or starve his royal stomach."

"Who knows?" whispered Sĕra, with an accent of awe. "They have never worked. Perhaps the gods supply their needs."

"Or they have robbed a tomb," returned Tadros. "It is much more likely; but if that is so I would like to find the place. There is money in a discovery of that sort. It means scarabs, and funeral idols, and amulets, and vases and utensils of olden days, all of which can be sold in Cairo for a good price. Sometimes it means jewels and gold ornaments as well; but that is only in the tombs of kings. Go to Hatatcha, my Sĕra, and keep your eyes open. Henf! what says the proverb? 'The outrunner of good fortune is thoughtfulness.'"

The mother of Nephthys nodded, and drew the last possible whiff from her cigarette. Then she left the hut and hurried under the heavy arch of Hatatcha's dwelling.

Five women, mostly old and all clothed in deep black, squatted in a circle around the rushes upon which lay the dead. Someone had closed Hatatcha's eyes, but otherwise she lay as she had expired. In a corner Kāra was chewing a piece of sugar-cane.

Sĕra joined the circle. She threw sand upon her head and wailed shrilly, rocking her body with a rhythmical motion. The others followed her example, and their cries were nerve-racking. Kāra looked at them a moment and then carried his sugar-cane out of doors.

For a time he stood still, hesitating. There was work for him to do, and he had only delayed it until the mourners were in possession of the house. But the sun was already hot and a journey lay before him. Kāra sighed. He was not used to work.

He walked to the north end of the huddle and entered the house of the blind man, Nikko. A Syrian donkey, with a long head and solemn eyes, stood near the door, and its owner was seated upon the ground rubbing its feet with an old rag that had been dipped in grease. Kāra caught up a bridle and threw it over the donkey's head.

"Who is it?" asked Nikko, turning his sightless eyes upward.

Kāra made no reply, but swung the saddle across the animal's back and tried to strap the girth. The old man twined his thin legs around those of the donkey and reached up a hand to pull the saddle away.

"It is Hatatcha's brute of a grandson!" cried Nikko, struggling to resist. "No other would try to rob me of my dear Mammek. Desist, or I will call the dragoman, who arrived this morning!"

For answer Kāra dealt him a kick in his stomach and he doubled up with a moan and rolled upon the ground. Then the royal one led Mammek out of the door and lightly leaped upon the donkey's back.

"Oo-ah!" he cried, digging his heels into the animal's flanks; and away trotted Mammek, meek but energetic.

There was no path in the direction he went and the desert sands seemed interminable. Kāra sat sidewise upon the donkey and sucked his sugar-cane, keeping the beast at a trot at the same time. An hour passed, and another. Finally a heap of rocky boulders arose just ahead of him, with a group of date palms at its foot. The heap grew bigger as he approached, and resolved itself into a small mountain, seared by deep fissures in the rocks. But there was verdure within the fissures, and several goats lay underneath the trees. Kāra rode past them and up to the foot of the mountain, where there was an overhanging entrance to a cave.

Throwing himself from the donkey, he ran into the cave and knelt at a spring which welled sparkling and cool from the rocks. Mammek followed and thrust his nozzle into the water beside Kāra's face. They drank together.

Then the man stood up and called aloud:

"Hi-yah, Sebbet; hi-yah!"

Someone laughed behind him, and Kāra swung upon his heel. There stood confronting him a curiously misshapen dwarf, whose snowy hair contrasted strangely with his dark chocolate skin. He was scarcely as tall as Kāra's waist, but his body and limbs were so enormous as to convey the impression of immense strength. He wore a spotless white burnous, which fell from his neck to his feet, but his head was bare of covering.

While the young man stared the dwarf spoke.

"I know your mission," said he, in ancient Egyptian. "Hatatcha is dead."

"It is true," returned Kāra, briefly.

"She swore I would live long enough to embalm her," continued the dwarf, rubbing his nose reflectively; "and she was right. A wonderful woman was old Hatatcha, and a royal one. I will keep my compact with her."

"Can you do it?" asked Kāra, wondering. "Do you know the ancient process of embalming?"

"Why, I am no paraschites, you understand, for the trade is without value in these degenerate days. But I successfully embalmed her mother—your great-grandmother—and Hatatcha was greatly pleased with the work. Does not your great-grandmother look natural? Have you seen her?"

Kāra shook his head.

"Not yet," he said.

"And I have safely hoarded the store of aromatic gums and spices, the palm wine and myrrh and cassia, and the natron, with which Hatatcha long since entrusted me. The strips of fine linen for the bandages and the urns for the entrails are still in my storehouse, where they have remained since your grandmother gave them into my hands; so there is no reason why her wishes should not be carried out."

"You will return with me?" asked Kāra.

"Yes, and bring the dead to this desolate spot," replied the dwarf. "It is no longer Hatatcha, but the envelope which she used, and will use again. Therefore it must be carefully preserved. The process will require forty days, as you know. At the end of that time I will deliver Hatatcha's mummy into your hands. You must then give to me a flat, oblong emerald that is graven with the cartouch of the mighty Ahtka-Rā. Is not that the compact, my prince?"

"It is, my Sebbet."

"And you know where to find it?" asked the dwarf, anxiously.

"I know," said Kāra.

The dwarf seemed pleased, and retired to make preparations for his journey. Kāra fell asleep in the cave, for the sun had been terribly hot and the long ride had exhausted him. The blind man's donkey also lay down and slept.

In the middle of the afternoon Sebbet awakened the young Egyptian and gave him some cakes to eat and a draught of goat's milk. Then he brought out a stout donkey of a pure white color and mounted it with unexpected agility. Kāra noticed a large sack fastened to the saddle-ring.

A moment later they were riding together across the sands.

"We must not reach Fedah before sundown," remarked the dwarf, and Kāra nodded assent. So they went at a moderate pace and bore the blistering rays of the sun as none but natives of Egypt can.

At sundown they sighted Gebel Abu Fedah, and it was dark when they entered the narrow street of Fedah. Kāra dismounted from Mammek's back at its master's hut, and at a slap on the thigh the donkey bolted quickly through the doorway. Then the young man followed after the dwarf to the threshold of his own dwelling.

The mourners had gone home and Hatatcha lay alone; but someone had placed a coarse cloth over her face to keep the flies away.

The dwarf drew from his pocket a rush-candle and lighted it. Removing the face-cloth he gazed for several minutes earnestly upon the features of the dead woman. Then he sighed deeply, untied the sack from his saddle and blew out the flame of the candle.

Kāra stood in the archway, looking at the slender rim of the moon. In a short time the dwarf's white donkey paused beside him. The sack, now bulky and

heavy, hung limply across the saddle. Kāra could see it plainly in the dim light.

He put his hand on the sack.

"Will it ride without tumbling off?" he asked.

"I will hold it fast," replied the dwarf, springing upon the donkey's back behind the burden. "Poor Hatatcha! She will not know we are taking our last ride together in Khonsu's company."

"Goodnight," said Kāra.

"Goodnight. In forty days, remember."

"In forty days."

"And the emerald?"

"You shall have it then."

The donkey hobbled out of the archway and passed silently down the little street. Presently it had faded into the night and was gone.

Kāra yawned and looked attentively at the huts. In only one, that of old Sĕra, a dim light burned. The man frowned, and then he laughed.

"Let the dragoman have his Nephthys," he muttered. "For me Cairo, London and the great world beckon. And women? Bah! There are women everywhere."

He entered the house and unrolled the mat that hung across the archway, fastening it securely to prevent intrusion.

IV

The Treasure of Ahtka-Rā

Kāra went to the cavity beside the arch and took from it a small bronze lamp. It was partly filled with oil, on the surface of which a cotton wick floated. The lamp itself was of quaint design, and the young man remembered it since the days of his childhood, but had rarely seen it in use.

Having lighted the wick and spread it with his fingers until it flamed up brightly, Kāra turned his back to the arch and carefully examined the rear wall of the room. The house, as has been explained, was built against a shallow cave of the mountains; but, owing to the irregularity of the hollow, part of the rear wall was of solid masonry, while the other part was formed by the cliff itself. Kāra had never before paid much attention to that fact, but now it struck him as very evident that the masonry had been constructed to shut off an orifice too deep or too irregular to be utilized as part of the dwelling. Otherwise, the continuation of the cliff would have rendered a wall unnecessary. The stones were of large size and were built up and cemented as far as the overhanging rock that formed the greater portion of the roof.

The Egyptian's eyes rested upon the third layer of these stones, and he counted from the corner to the seventh stone. In appearance this was not different from the others; but Hatatcha's directions had been exact, and she knew.

He walked to the spot and pressed hard against the right edge of the stone. It moved, and gradually swung inward, the left edge being supported by solid pivots of bronze at the top and bottom.

The opening disclosed was about four feet long by three feet in height, and Kāra at once crept through it, holding his lamp extended before him. Yes; his surmise had been correct—a low, but deep and irregular cavern was behind the wall.

His first care was to close up the entrance by pressing the block of stone back to its former position. There was a bronze handle on the inner side that would permit him to open it again easily.

The cavern felt damp and cool, and when he raised his lamp he saw some deep fissures leading far under the mountain. He selected the second from the left of these rifts and cautiously made his way along the rough floor. At first it seemed that he had made a mistake, for this way was less promising than several of the others; but when he stopped and thought upon Hatatcha's directions, he knew that he was right.

The rift made a sudden turn and sank downward; but the rocks under his feet were now more even and the way became easier to traverse. A hundred paces farther, the passage ended abruptly in a sharp point where the rock had originally split.

The young Egyptian walked to the extreme end and then carefully measured three paces back again. Raising his lamp, he examined the right wall of the tunnel closely. It contained many irregular cracks and hollows, but one indentation seemed, on observation, to be surrounded by a tiny circle of black, or a color darker than the other portions of the rock.

Kāra uttered an exclamation of pleasure. He had feared he might not find this spot, in spite of his grandmother's assurances that it was plain to keen eyes.

Drawing a short, pointed dagger from the folds of his burnous—a weapon he had found in the crypt beside the arch of the living-room—the Egyptian thrust it into the orifice of the rock and pushed until it had sunk in to the very hilt. Then he turned the handle, and a sharp "click" was audible.

Kāra stepped back a pace, and a part of the rock, circular in shape, swung slowly out into the passage, revealing another tunnel running at right angles with the first. Unlike the other, this was no natural fissure of the rock, but an excavation cleverly made by the hands of man. The roof was arched and the floor level and smooth.

The man slipped through the opening and proceeded along the arched passage. He did not close this door behind him, for Hatatcha had warned him not to do so. The floor had a gradual slope and he knew that he was going still farther beneath the mountain at every step. The atmosphere now became hot and stifling and he found it difficult to breathe; but he continued steadily walking for a matter of five minutes—which seemed an hour—holding the lamp before him, until finally he noticed the blaze of the wick flicker, as if a breath of fresher air had reached it.

By this time his breast had seemed ready to burst, and his breathing was fitful and gasping; but he hurried forward and now found the air cooler and fresher and drew it into his lungs gratefully.

The path was no longer downward, and before him he presently discovered a huge pillar of rock, which at first sight seemed to block the tunnel. Rude hieroglyphics were graven upon it. Passing around this at the left, he found himself in a high, vaulted chamber, and stopped with a sigh of satisfaction.

The chamber was circular in shape, and not more than sixteen feet in diameter. An air-shaft in the dome evidently led to some part of the summit of the mountain, for Kāra found himself breathing naturally again.

"This," said he, "must be the library that Hatatcha mentioned."

All around the walls of the vault were niches, cut in regular rows and containing box-like receptacles covered with inscriptions and pictures in gaudy colors. In the center of the room stood a large round slab of granite, finely polished upon its upper surface.

Kāra drew a box from its niche and set it upon the granite slab beside his lamp. Then he took from it a roll of papyrus, which he examined with interest.

Yes; he had read it before. It was one of those so often mysteriously produced by his grandmother to assist in his education. He examined another roll, and a third, leisurely and with care. These also he knew well. There were two hundred and eighteen rolls of papyrus in this ancient library, and the knowledge they contained had all been absorbed by the young Egyptian years before. He read them easily, and knew at once from their context the different meanings of many signs that are yet puzzling less-favored students of the hieroglyphics.

The manuscripts dated from the fourth dynasty down to the days of the Ptolemies, and, in a large cavity below the rolls of papyrus, were ranged the earlier works of Herodotus, Diodorus Siculus, Manetho, Horapello, Strabo and others, as well as the volumes on modern Egyptian and European history that old Hatatcha had purchased in Cairo within the last few years. Several historical stelæ of the earlier kings of Egypt also leaned against the walls, arranged in chronological order, and this library, founded by Ahtka-Rā, which had been preserved and added to for so many centuries, was a veritable storehouse of the records of his remarkable country.

Kāra smiled queerly as he glanced around the room.

"Others argue concerning ancient Egypt," he muttered; "but I alone know the truth."

A pile of papyrus rolls in another cavity seemed of less importance than those so carefully arranged in boxes. Kāra brought an armful of them to the central slab, dusted them with his rope, and selected fifteen of their number after a cursory glance at their contents. The others he restored to their place. This being accomplished, he took up his lamp and returned to the passage, this time circling the pillar of rock to the right.

It led into an immense oblong chamber, so vast that the light of Kāra's bronze lamp seemed to penetrate the blackness but a few feet in advance. But other lamps were suspended from huge bronze brackets, and several of these the Egyptian proceeded to light, finding them nearly all supplied with oil.

Then, stepping backward, he gazed about him with an irrepressible sensation of awe. The huge chamber was filled with mummy-cases, arranged upon solid slabs of Aswan granite. Nearest to the entrance were a dozen or so slabs that were unoccupied. Then appeared a splendid case of solid ebony, elaborately carved upon every inch of its surfaces. This had been made for Hatatcha in London, during her residence in that city, and secretly transported to this place by devices only known to her. The inscriptions were all in the sign language except the one word, "Hatatcha," which appeared in Roman letters upon the cover. It was empty, of course, and Kāra proceeded to the next slab. Upon it lay the mummy of his great-grandmother, Thi-Aten, the one so naturally embalmed by the dwarf Sebbet. Her limbs were bandaged separately and the contour of her face might be clearly seen through the thin and tightly-drawn linen that covered it. Kāra sighed and made a profound obeisance to the mummy before proceeding up the chamber.

As he advanced, the mummies increased in age and also in the magnificence of their cases and the importance of their inscriptions. Some of the slabs were covered thickly with hieroglyphics relating the life history of their occupants, while on them were crowded curious ushabtiu figures, amulets and scarabs. Finally Kāra reached the end of the chamber and paused beside the mummy of the great Ahtka-Rā, who, while not king in name, had nevertheless ruled Egypt during his lifetime through the weak Rameses II, whom men ignorantly call "the Great."

Long the Egyptian knelt before the remains of his great ancestor. Rameses himself, and Seti his father, and many other kings of Egypt were lying in the museum at Cairo, to be impudently stared at by crowds of curious modern tourists; but this famous one had wisely provided for his own seclusion and that of his posterity. It was

Ahtka-Rā who had constructed this hidden tomb during his lifetime, and he kept the secret so well that no painted or graven record of it existed to guide a meddling foreign race to its discovery in the years that were to come.

Kāra's eyes fairly gloated upon the mummy case of his wonderful ancestor. It was studded thick with precious stones, any of which might be deemed a fortune to one who, like himself, had existed so long in a lowly condition. But he did not disturb these gems. Instead, he touched a spring in the slab, a portion of which slid forward and revealed an opening.

Kāra took his lamp and crept into the aperture. There were seventeen steps leading downward; then came a short passage, and he entered another large chamber hewn from the solid rock.

Here was the treasure house of Ahtka-Rā, its contents doubtless primarily rifled from the treasure cities of Pithom and Raamses, which after his death were found to have been despoiled.

The entire room was faced with polished granite, and around the walls were granite tables to hold the treasure, as well as immense wide-mouthed vases of porphyry, malachite, lapis lazuli, carnelian and bronze. Upon the tables were heaps of chains, bracelets, ornaments and utensils of pure gold. In the center of the room stood twelve alabaster pedestals, two rows of six each, and each pedestal supported a splendid vase containing gems of various sorts. On the floor were numerous other vases and receptacles for jewels and golden ornaments, and one of these Kāra noticed was yet more than half filled with the precious coins of Darius Hystaspes, some of which his grandmother had used to provide herself with necessities because they were of a comparatively modern date and would arouse no suspicion that the source of their supply was the ancient tomb of Ahtka-Rā.

Indeed, it was easy to be seen that many of Ahtka-Rā's successors had added to this treasure house instead of pilfering from it. The original store, contained in the twelve great malachite vases, was practically untouched, although Hatatcha must have drawn upon it at one time. All the treasure littering the tables and floor had been added since Ahtka-Rā had lain in his tomb.

Kāra's face was unmoved, but his eyes glistened brightly. He thrust his hand into a jar and drew it out filled with rubies. They were of all sizes and shades of coloring and were polished in flat surfaces instead of being cut into rose facets according to modern methods. Some of the stones had small characters graven upon them, but usually they were smoothly polished.

The Egyptian now turned to the wall tables. Here were also rubies, diamonds, amethysts and emeralds, set in golden ornaments of many designs. Some of the stones were of so great a size as to be extremely valuable. A casket of dark wood inlaid with silver hieroglyphics attracted Kāra's attention. He threw back the lid and took from it a massive chain of gold, which he threw over his head. Each link was finely engraved with characters relating the name of some king and a deed he had accomplished. Kāra read some of the inscriptions and was amazed. The chain had originally been made in twelve links by Bā-en-nĕter, the twelfth king dating from Mēnēs, during whose reign the Nile flowed honey for eleven days. His successor, Uătch-nēs, took the chain and added another link, and so the chain had grown through succeeding ages down to the time of Ahtka-Rā. No wonder it was long and heavy!

Kāra did not like to replace this marvelous chain. He dropped its links inside his burnous and left it hanging around his neck.

After an hour or more devoted to the inspection of these treasures, which the young man naturally regarded as his own, forgetting that Hatatcha had warned him he but held them in trust, Kāra reluctantly prepared to leave the chamber. First, however, he selected twenty-three great diamonds from a jar and concealed them in the folds of his turban. The turban is called the Egyptian's pocket, because a burnous seldom has pockets, and many things can be secreted in the voluminous cloth of a turban.

"Here is one diamond for every year I have lived," said Kāra. "Surely I am entitled to that many."

But it did not satisfy him. He thrust his hand into the jar of rubies again and took all that his fingers could clutch. He loved the color of the rubies. They appealed to him.

Then he crept up the stairs, reëntered the mummy chamber, and closed the secret slide in the malachite slab upon which lay the mighty Ahtka-Rā.

Who, not initiated, would ever suspect the enormous wealth lying so close at hand? Kāra sighed deeply and held himself proudly erect. He was just beginning to realize his own importance.

Extinguishing the lights of the lamps he had kindled in this chamber, he retraced his steps to the library, where he gathered up the fifteen rolls of papyrus, carrying them in the front breadth of his burnous while he held fast to the hem. In this way he returned along the arched passage until he came to the rock door which he had left ajar. He climbed through the opening and thrust the rock back into place, listening while the heavy bolt fastened itself with a sharp click.

He was now in the natural fissure of the mountain cavern, and it did not take him long to reach the stone wall which alone separated him from Hatatcha's dwelling.

He paused a moment, with his ear to the wall; but hearing no sound, he extinguished his light and then caught the handle imbedded in the stone and swung the block upon its pivots. In a moment he was in the living-room, and the wall through which he had passed seemed solid and immovable.

He must have been absent for several hours during his exploring expedition into the mountain, and the night was now far advanced.

Kāra flung the papyri into a corner, covered them with loose rushes from his grandmother's couch, and then threw himself upon his own bed to sleep. He had been awake the better part of two nights, and his eyelids were as heavy as if weighted with lead.

V

A Roll of Papyrus

At daybreak the dragoman thrust his head stealthily through the arch and looked at Kāra's sleeping form with suspicion. He had visited the young man's house in the evening and found him absent and Hatatcha's body also gone. He came again later, and once more at midnight, and still Hatatcha's dead form and her grandson's quick one were alike missing.

Then the dragoman, wishing to know to what secret place the old woman's remains had been taken, and from which direction Kāra returned, and having a fair share of oriental shrewdness, had stretched two threads across the narrow street—one on either side the arch—and afterward returned to his couch in the house of old Sĕra to sleep.

Daybreak found him awake and stirring. He discovered both his threads unbroken, yet the young Egyptian was sound asleep within the room. The dragoman scratched his left ear in perplexity and shook his head. Kāra was doubtless clever, but his unusual actions led Tadros to believe there was something important afoot. And that matter of the coins and the ancient jewel of old Hatatcha was well worth investigating.

He sat down cross-legged in the cool arch and waited. Kāra slept on. The girl Nephthys brought the dragoman a cake for his breakfast, silently placed it in his hand, and carried her jar to the river. On her return she paused to allow her master to drink and then left him again.

Tadros lighted a cigarette and smoked it to the end. Then he pushed aside the mat and looked into the room long and steadily. Kāra lay like one dead; in some strange manner the lazy one must have exhausted his strength—perhaps in carrying his grandmother's corpse to some far-away tomb. Ah, that was the secret place, doubtless, from whence the coins and the jewel had come. Kāra must know of it, and therefore it would be well for Tadros to win his confidence. What was that heap of rushes in the corner, and why had they been taken from Hatatcha's former couch? The dragoman was suddenly interested. He unfastened a portion of the mat and crept into the room. Kāra did not hear him. Softly he advanced on hands and knees to the corner. He felt among the rushes and drew out a roll of papyrus.

For a moment the dragoman sat still, his heart beating wildly. Here was a find, indeed! He knew of a dozen scholars who would willingly bankrupt themselves to discover a new papyrus roll.

He crawled slowly back to the arch and seated himself where a ray of light came between the mat and the gray stones. Here he unrolled the manuscript and examined it eagerly. He did not claim to be much of a student, but he could read hieroglyphics a little and was a judge of ancient picture-writing. Here was doubtless a scroll of great antiquity and value, relating incidents of the war of Rameses against the Kheta, and its state of preservation was wonderful. In this place was a list of captives brought back to Thebes; in that was the expense account of the army. Here was told the—

"Henf!"

The sharp, quick cry was followed by a sudden rustle of the rushes, and with a spring like that of a panther, Kāra was upon the impudent intruder into his domain. Before Tadros could rise, his assailant was kneeling upon his body and with lithe, delicate fingers clutching viciously at his throat. The dragoman struggled to free himself, but could not. He tried to breathe, without effect. The skin of his bronzed face grew black, and his eyes protruded from their sockets with a look of horror and fear.

Seeing this, Kāra's set face suddenly relaxed and lost its look of murderous determination. He released his hold of the dragoman and pushed away the mat to allow more air to get to him.

Slowly the other, gasping and uttering low moans, recovered his breath. Kāra's fingers had left great discoloured blotches upon his neck; but that did not matter. From certain death he was coming back to life, and the transition was one to evoke gratitude and joy. Life was sweet to the dragoman—the sweetest thing he possessed.

Kāra, standing erect, looked down upon him with arms folded in repose and a countenance very thoughtful. Two reasons had stayed his vengeful hands. To murder Tadros would get him into trouble with the authorities, and so cause him great annoyance at this critical juncture, when liberty of action and freedom from espionage was important. In the second place, his half-formed plans included the use of the dragoman for his own advantage. Tadros was both clever and well known. He would become a good servant when he knew it would further his personal interest to be faithful, and so it was best that the dragoman should live—for a time.

He had now almost recovered from the shock of Kāra's assault, and began to grow angry.

"What do you mean, you dog, by felling me like a wild beast and trying to throttle me?" he demanded, with his first breath.

"What do you mean by stealing into my house and prying into my private affairs?" returned Kāra brusquely.

The dragoman's eyes fell upon the papyrus at his feet, and his face changed its expression.

"Where did you get it?" he asked, quickly. "Are there more of them? Is it a tomb or a temple? Tell me, Kāra, tell me all about it."

The Egyptian smiled, grimly.

"There are more of them," he said. "Look! in that corner are fourteen other rolls; but whether they came from a tomb or a temple I do not know. They are my inheritance from Hatatcha. Where she found them she alone could have told; but she carried the secret to the nether world."

Tadros mused for a time.

"Where have they been kept all these years?" he asked in a tone of disbelief.

"Hidden underneath the rushes of her bed. I dragged them all out last night, as you can see."

"Were there anymore of the coins?"

"A few." He showed some in his hand.

"Ah!"

The dragoman drew a deep breath.

"You are rich, my prince," said he. "Fifteen papyri of the ancient days!—they are worth a fortune in any event."

"How much?" asked Kāra, amused.

"This one," said Tadros, picking it up and partly unrolling it to glance again at the writing, "I could sell in Cairo for five hundred piastres— perhaps a thousand. It is wonderfully clear and well preserved."

"You may keep it for yourself," said Kāra.

Tadros stared.

"I will exchange it for the girl Nephthys," continued the young man, coolly. "For her you have paid to old Sĕra two hundred and fifty piastres already. You must pay a like sum to take the girl away with you, and afterward you must pay for her support. Very well; I will relieve you of the burden. You will not only save your money, but you will get a papyrus worth four times what you have invested."

Tadros frowned and looked glum.

"But the girl is mine!" he exclaimed.

"And the papyrus is mine," returned Kāra. "Perhaps I could buy two or three like Nephthys with it; but never mind, it shall be yours in the way of exchange."

Tadros moved uneasily and cast a longing glance at the roll.

"I like not this barbaric traffic in womankind," he muttered, with indecision.

"Nor I," agreed Kāra. "It is Sĕra who is to blame. If she has a fat daughter, she will want a fat price for her. Otherwise, how can she be recompensed for the girl's keep? But five hundred is too much for Nephthys. I would have to give her mother the other two hundred and fifty piastres myself—and you would have the roll. By Isis, 'tis a bad bargain! Here; let us say no more about it. Give me the papyrus."

"Wait—wait!" cried Tadros. "Why are you so unjust in your conclusions? The bargain is made. No one but a sneaking Arab goes back on his word."

"It is as you say," replied Kāra, stretching his long arms and yawning. "But it is a fine papyrus, Tadros—all about the Kheta and King Rameses."

"I know; I know!" returned the dragoman, nervously tucking his prize under his arm. "Come with me at once. I will inform Sĕra of the transfer of my property."

He rose to his feet a little unsteadily, because his throat still hurt him, and led the way.

Kāra quietly followed.

In Sĕra's hovel mother and daughter were weaving upon a rude cane loom.

"See here," announced the dragoman; "this Nephthys is too free with her favors, and I cannot be coming forever to this forsaken village to look after her. Besides, I must get back to Cairo to attend to my business, so I have sold the girl to my friend Kāra here, and when he takes her away from you, if ever he does, he is to pay the other two hundred and fifty piastres I promised."

Sĕra seemed surprised, but nodded her head cheerfully.

"It is all the same to me," she replied. "If the royal one has the money to satisfy you, it is none of my business, I am sure. An alliance with the descendant of the great Ahtka-Rā is something to be proud of."

The girl had broken a thread. As she prepared to retie it, she glanced from one to the other of the two men with a look of indifference.

"I do not promise to make Nephthys a wife," said Kāra, slowly, "although, of course, it may come to that. My plans are not formed for the future. But I have acquired the girl in betrothal through my compact with Tadros, and his rights are hereafter mine."

"She grows plumper everyday," said Sĕra, glancing at Nephthys critically. "You will seek long, my Kāra, before you find a more desirable wife. Yet I am in no hurry to lose my daughter, believe me, even for the money she will bring. Take your time about deciding the matter."

"I will," responded Kāra, briefly.

"And now, tell me, what has become of your grandmother, Hatatcha?"

"I have carried her into the desert to be embalmed."

And then, to avoid further questioning, he went away.

VI

KĀRA BATHES IN THE NILE

T adros followed him into the street again.

"Those other papyri," he said—"do you wish me to sell them for you?"

"They are already sold," replied Kāra, regardless of truth.

"Indeed! To whom?"

"Winston Bey, the Englishman."

Tadros uttered an exclamation of annoyance.

"Where have you met him?" he asked.

"Here, at the Nile landing. His boat will come tonight for the papyrus rolls."

Many thoughts passed rapidly through the dragoman's mind. Here was bad news, indeed. He had planned on getting all those wonderful rolls into his own hands, and his disappointment was keen to find that this isolated Egyptian of an out-of-the-way rock village had already been approached and bought up by one of those rascally scientists, before he, the clever dragoman, had even known of the existence of the treasures.

"He will rob you," he ventured to suggest.

"Very well," replied Kāra, indifferently.

Tadros was in despair. Yet one thing was plainly evident—if Winston Bey was about to unload fourteen newly found rolls of papyrus upon the directors of the museum in Cairo, it would be well for him, the dragoman, to get his one roll in first, at the highest possible price. That could easily be accomplished. Winston's dahabeah would consume four or five days on the downward voyage. Tadros could cross the Nile in a small boat and catch the railway on the other bank, which would land him in Cairo the next day. He promptly decided to take the railway.

"I expect," said Kāra, "to be in Cairo myself shortly. If you are there, I would like to hire your services as dragoman."

Tadros, aroused from his meditations, gave a start, and wonderingly examined the speaker from his dirty bare feet all the way up his soiled burnous to his strong, calm face and faded turban. He had been a native of Fedah himself, and had known "the royal one," as he scornfully called

Kāra, from boyhood. Until now he had regarded him as a permanent fixture of the little village; a listless, lazy do-nothing, supported in some mysterious way by his grandmother and destined to grow old amid his solitary surroundings.

Some slight importance Kāra had doubtless acquired through his inheritance of the papyri; but that he should think of visiting Cairo and employing the brilliantly appareled dragoman was a marvel that fairly astounded Tadros. Yet, why not? He would have money. Tadros could assuredly teach him how to spend it. Kāra might become an incident in his career—an element in his future prosperity.

"Call upon me at anytime," he said, condescendingly. "You shall have the advantage of my experience and knowledge of the world."

"That is what I want," returned the Egyptian, "and I will pay you liberally for it."

He passed into his dwelling, and the dragoman, watching him go, decided to make speedy preparation for his own departure.

He felt much easier in his mind than at first. What if Winston Bey purchased the papyrus rolls? Would not Tadros be the young man's guide? Very good. Very good, indeed!

Kāra lay down again and slept until after noon. Then he went to the hut of Nefert, who baked the bread for the village, and bargained with her for a loaf and a bowl of milk. Also he acquired from her a large, coarse sack. In exchange he gave her Hatatcha's water jar, which had come from Keneh, and an old scarf his grandmother had worn over her head.

He ate the loaf and drank the milk, feeling much refreshed. Then he carried the sack to his dwelling and placed the papyrus rolls in it.

From the secret cavity beside the arch he took the bronze vase with the metal stopper, a scarab ring that his grandmother had sometimes worn, and a slender dagger with a steel blade. The bronze dagger that served as a key to the rock door he left in the cavity, as well as the lamp.

Having replaced the stone, he glanced around to see whether there was anything that might be disturbed or stolen during his absence; but the room was bare of anything to tempt a thief or a despoiler. So he swung the sack over his shoulder and walked out and around the end of the mountain on his way to the Nile.

Winston Bey had kept his word. On the chance that the strange Egyptian he had encountered would manage to secure either valuable information or some ancient relics from his mysterious grandmother, he had kept his dahabeah in the neighborhood, ignoring the protests of his unhappy Arab crew. The afternoon following his interview with Kāra, he landed near the group of palms an hour before sunset, and waited until darkness fell without obtaining a sight of the Egyptian. Then he dropped down the stream to Tel El Armana, where the dahabeah remained until the next noon.

Today he figured on another disappointment; but when Gerald Winston had an object in view he pursued it with dogged determination, and he had resolved to keep his appointment each day for a week at least before considering his future actions. There was no question but he was on the track of an important discovery, and he did not intend to abandon the quest lightly.

On this second day, therefore, when he approached the grove and saw a white-robed figure sitting in the shade, his heart gave a joyful bound. He hurried forward and recognized Kāra, who remained motionless until the Englishman had saluted him. Then he bowed his head gravely.

Winston's eyes were on the sack that rested beside the Egyptian, and his voice sounded eager in spite of his effort to restrain it.

"Well, my brother?" he exclaimed.

"My grandmother, Hatatcha, is dead," said Kāra.

The Englishman shrank back in horror.

"You have killed her?"

"Oh, no; not at all," answered the other composedly. "She was dying when I returned home after my conversation with you. It would not pay me to kill Hatatcha, you know."

"What did you learn from her?"

"Nothing. She was beyond questioning. But she whispered that I should seek under the rushes of her bed for my inheritance, and then Anubis took her to his kingdom. Her secret, if she had one, she carried with her."

Winston was deeply chagrined. He reproached himself for not having interviewed the old woman in person and endeavored to wrest her secret from her. Now, alas, it was too late!

"What have you in the sack?" he inquired, almost indifferently.

"My inheritance," said Kāra.

"Of what does it consist?"

"I have fourteen rolls of ancient papyrus manuscript."

"Fourteen rolls?" cried Winston, trembling with sudden excitement. "Let me see them, man—let me see them!"

Kāra did not move.

"I am going to Cairo," said he. "Will you take me with you in your boat?"

"Yes; to be sure. Come to the boat at once."

"That is better," declared the Egyptian. "You can then examine the papyri at your leisure and determine whether they are of interest to you."

He slowly arose to his feet and swung the sack across his shoulder. Winston eagerly preceded him. The stifling heat was all forgotten. Hatatcha's unfortunate death was forgotten. A treasure had been unearthed at last, and surely from fourteen manuscripts much important information might be gleaned.

On the deck of his dahabeah he glanced at the papyri with amazement. Each one was perfectly preserved and unrolled without danger of breaking.

"Their condition is extraordinary!" he observed. "Where, did you say, you found them?"

"In a hollow of earth, covered by the rushes of Hatatcha's couch."

Winston raised his head to look at the speaker closely.

"Then they have not been there long, I am sure."

"That," said Kāra, with a shrug, "is a matter of which I have no knowledge."

The scientist carefully unrolled a manuscript.

"This," he said, musingly, "is a poem by the poet Pen-ta-urt. And it is a composition I have never seen before."

He began reading it, and soon Kāra corrected him in a passage and explained how he should properly translate it. Winston's eyes sparkled. This Egyptian really knew the hieroglyphics better than he did. His assistance might be invaluable in some ways. Perhaps the man would prove as remarkable a find as the manuscripts.

The next writing was an address to his soldiers by Amenhotep III, on the eve of his invasion of Syria. It was beautifully executed, and would prove a valuable addition to the literature of the fifteenth century before Christ.

Far into the night Winston pored over the writings, finding in some veritable treasures and in others little of worth save for their age and beauty of execution. Still, as a collection, the fourteen rolls constituted a remarkable library of ancient literature, and its fortunate discoverer slept but little on that eventful night.

Before daybreak the dahabeah was wheezing and puffing down

stream on its way to Cairo, and Kāra, who had slept well extended upon the deck, was given a breakfast such as he had never before tasted. The fragrant coffee was a revelation to him, and the chops and fruit made his eyes sparkle; yet so sedate was the Egyptian's demeanor that Winston was unaware that his guest had never before eaten a properly prepared meal.

The Englishman's satisfaction this morning was so great that he also bestowed upon Kāra one of his choicest cigars, and again the Egyptian tasted a luxury hitherto unknown to him.

While they were quietly enjoying their smoke Winston said:

"Will you sell me the rolls?"

"Yes," replied Kāra.

"I will give you a thousand Egyptian pounds for them. That, you know, is about a hundred thousand piastres."

Kāra made a mental calculation and frowned darkly.

"Perhaps it is not enough," added Winston, quickly; "but on the other hand it may be too much altogether. Until I have examined the writings with more care I cannot value them accurately."

"I will accept your offer," said the Egyptian, still frowning. "I am sure it is fair, and even liberal. What annoys me is that I have made a fool of myself."

"In what way?"

"I purchased a girl yesterday, and paid three times what she is worth."

Winston smiled.

"Do not let it bother you," he said, in an amused tone. "Few women are worth what they cost, believe me, and where their sex is concerned men are often fools."

"My brother's speech is wise," returned the grave Kāra. "I will conceal my annoyance, for some day I may be indemnified."

"Had Hatatcha any of the coins of Darius Hystaspes left?" inquired Winston, after a moment's thought.

"Here are seven," said the other, producing them.

The Englishman was delighted.

"I will pay you five pounds each for these," said he.

"Then they are yours," declared Kāra.

Afterward he showed the Englishman the bronze vase, which also changed hands at a liberal purchase price.

"And is this all?" asked Winston.

"It is all," said Kāra.

"You will be rich, my brother. Here are ten pounds in English gold to seal our bargain. After we arrive in Cairo I will take you to my banker and transfer to your account the entire amount due you. You may draw then upon the bank as you require your money, in any sums that suit your convenience—so long as it lasts."

"I thank you," replied the Egyptian.

As they proceeded down the river, Kāra noted the spotless tunics and trousers of the Arabs, who one and all regarded "the dirty Copt" with open contempt. He also examined intently the Englishman's dress. When the boat tied up at Assyut to allow Winston to visit a friend who was convalescent at the excellent hospital maintained there, Kāra walked through the bazaars, and returned to the dahabeah bearing several bulky packages.

That night he bathed in the river while the others all lay asleep. Afterward he stealthily transferred the contents of his turban to a chamois bag, which he fastened around his neck. Then he flung the old burnous and the turban overboard.

In the morning they found the Egyptian transformed. He wore an English shirt, with collar and necktie all of white, loose linen trousers that were gathered at the ankles in Arab style, and over these a flowing white burnous of spotless purity. Upon his head was a red fez; upon his feet red slippers from Algiers; about his neck hung the massive chain of the kings; upon his finger was his grandmother's ring set with the scarab of Ahtka-Rā.

Winston was astonished, and gazed upon the Egyptian with approval. Then his eye caught the chain, and he uttered an exclamation of wonder.

"Where did you get it?" he asked, clutching at the chain to examine one of its exquisitely engraved links.

"It is also a part of my inheritance, but an heirloom that I dare not part with," returned Kāra. "It is the record of the kings, my ancestors, from Mēnēs to Ahtka-Rā," and he explained the meaning of the chain to Winston, and assisted him to decipher some of the inscriptions upon the heavy links.

"But this is a priceless treasure!" exclaimed the savant, filled with unbounded amazement at what he beheld.

"It is proof of my contention that I am of royal blood," answered the other, proudly. "While I live I will not be separated from it."

"You are right," agreed Winston, promptly; and from that moment he entertained a new respect for this humble descendant of the ancient rulers of Egypt.

Not one of the manuscripts mentioned Ahtka-Rā; but the chain had at its end the link of that astute leader of men, and his identity was thus established beyond a doubt. The scarab, of unquestionable antiquity, was likewise a proof that Kāra's ancestor was a descendant of kings. Immediately the young Egyptian became a person of consequence.

Kāra now smoked cigarettes, having purchased several boxes at Assyut. This was the most satisfactory luxury that attended his new condition, and conspired, more than anything else, to render him pleased with his lot.

The dahabeah arrived in Cairo on the morning of the fourth day.

Winston at once took a carriage and drove Kāra to the bank, where he placed the sum agreed upon to the young Egyptian's credit. Kāra, who wrote English in a clear and delicate hand, was given a cheque book and registered his signature as follows: "Prince Kāra."

"Residence?" inquired the banker.

"I have just arrived, and am not yet located," was the answer. "Tomorrow I will send you my address."

"Let me also know where you are to be found," said Winston, "for I must introduce you to the Egyptologists here."

Then he left his new acquaintance to drive post haste to the museum, there to show his new-found treasures to his many friends.

VII

A Step Toward the Goal

Kāra wandered about the streets. Cairo is a marvel to the most blasé traveler; it could not fail to impress an inexperienced native. But the Egyptian masked the astonishment under an expression cold and reserved and a manner dignified and undemonstrative. No one must suspect he was fresh from the desert and the Nile country. The shops of the jewelers especially attracted his attention, and he stopped many times to examine the splendid gems displayed in the windows. Some were priced, and he wondered at their value. It is said that no capital in the world contains so many rare and costly gems as Cairo.

In the evening he crossed the great bridge of Isma'il Pasha to the island of Gizireh, staring at the procession of carriages, camels, automobiles and donkeys that at twilight followed on one another's heels. In the carriages and automobiles rode Syrians, Turks, Copts and Arabs, clothed in conventional European dress, save for the red fez everywhere prevalent. The burnous and native dress had been abandoned by these aristocrats, and this met with Kāra's full approval. He was not averse to innovations upon the ancient customs in which he had been reared. If the dominant people of his country and age were English, then the manners and customs of the English should be adopted by those who wished to compete with them in importance.

Also he began to understand that it is more dignified to ride than to walk. At Gizireh he hailed a carriage and in it returned across the bridge, avoiding the dust and heat and mingling with a procession of beautifully costumed women and handsomely dressed men. His own costume was poor enough in comparison, but his magnificent chain drew the eye of more than one curious observer.

And now Cairo was ablaze with lights, and the population seemed gathered upon the sidewalks before the cafés and restaurants. Kāra discovered that he was hungry. He dismissed his carriage and seated himself at one of the outdoor tables, ordering liberal refreshment. Opposite him sat a young English girl with a vacant-faced man for escort. Kāra, as he ate, examined this girl critically, for she was the first of her class he had seen at close range. Her dress was dainty and beautiful; but she was not fat at all. She was vivacious, and talked and laughed with unrestrained liberty. She seemed to imagine herself on an equality with the man beside her, who, despite his inanity, was still a man. Altogether, Kāra was disappointed in her, although his grandmother had warned him that the training of European women imbued them with peculiar ideas, to which he must defer in his association with them.

As he watched the girl, Nephthys rose several degrees in Kāra's estimation. Nephthys was certainly

fat and soft of flesh, and she did not talk much. The possession of such a woman was quite desirable, and perhaps he had not paid an extravagant price for Nephthys after all. These independent, chattering Western women must be tolerated, however, until he had accomplished his mission; so it would be well to begin at once to study their ways.

Presently someone touched his shoulder familiarly, causing Kāra to shrink back with an indignant gesture. Tadros, the dragoman, stood smilingly beside him, more gorgeously arrayed than ever. Tadros was in an excellent humor. He had not been obliged to take his roll of papyrus to the museum for a market, but had disposed of it to a private collector for a price far exceeding his expectations, which had not been too modest. Altogether he had made an excellent trade, and there might be other pickings in this unsophisticated fellow-townsman of his, whose very presence in Cairo was warrant that he had money to part with.

Before accosting Kāra the dragoman had observed the change in his appearance and demeanor. The former recluse was no longer disgustingly filthy, but seemed clean in person and was gowned in a snowy and respectable burnous. The objectionable turban had given place to the fez; the red slippers were of excellent morocco. Best of all, the chain around his neck was rich and heavy and of remarkable workmanship. Kāra was not only presentable, but his manner was dignified and well bred.

All this indicated suddenly acquired wealth—that mysterious old Hatatcha must have left to her grandson much more than the papyrus rolls; and although Kāra might endeavor to be secret and uncommunicative, he was bound to betray himself before very long. Now was the heated term, and even gay Cairo was listless and enervated. The dragoman would have ample leisure to pick this bone skilfully before the tourist season arrived.

Kāra's first angry exclamation was followed by a word of greeting. He was glad Tadros had found him, for as yet he had secured no place of residence, and the bigness of the city somewhat bewildered him in spite of his assumed reserve.

The dragoman agreed to take him to a respectable rooming-house much frequented by Copts of the better class. When they had arrived there, Kāra's guide made a mystic sign to the proprietor, who promptly charged his new guest double the usual rate, and obtained it because the Egyptian was unaware he was being robbed. The room assigned him was a simply furnished, box-like affair; yet Kāra had never before occupied an apartment so luxurious. He examined the door with care and was pleased to find that it was supplied with a stout bolt as well as a lock and key.

"Now," said the dragoman, "it is yet early; we have barely crossed the edge of the evening. I will take you to the theatre to see the dancing girls, and later to a house where they wager money upon a singular and interesting game of red and black. We can afterward eat our supper at a restaurant and listen to a fine band composed of Hungarian gypsies. How will that suit you?"

"Not at all," replied Kāra, coldly. "I am going to bed. Be here to receive my orders at seven o'clock in the morning."

Tadros fairly gasped with astonishment.

"Seven o'clock is too early," he said, a little sullenly. "The city is asleep at that hour."

"When does it awaken?"

"Well, the shops are open at about nine."

"Come to me, then, at nine. Goodnight."

This summary dismissal was a severe disappointment to the dragoman, yet he had no alternative but to take his leave. Strange that Kāra had refused the dancing girls and the game table; but perhaps he was really tired. Tadros must not expect too much from his innocent at first.

At nine o'clock the next morning he found that the young Egyptian had breakfasted and was impatiently awaiting him.

"Take me to the leading jeweler in town," said Kāra.

The dragoman frowned, but presently brightened again and took his employer to a second-rate shop, where his commissions were assured.

"Not here," said Kāra. "I have seen much better shops."

Tadros tried again, but with no better success; so he altered his plans and took Kāra direct to Andalaft's, trusting to luck to exact a commission afterward.

"Now, then," said he, briskly, "what shall we examine first?"

But Kāra ignored him, asking to see the proprietor in private. Mr. Andalaft graciously consented to the interview, and when the Egyptian entered the great jeweler's private room Tadros was left outside.

Kāra laid a splendid ruby upon the merchant's table. The latter pounced upon it with an eager exclamation.

"It is very old," said the Egyptian. "Tell me, sir, is there anyone in Cairo who can recut it in the modern fashion?"

"But it will be a shame to alter this exquisite gem," protested Andalaft. "It is the square, flat cutting of the ancients, and shows the stone to be absolutely pure and flawless. Such specimens are rare in these days. Let it alone."

Kāra shook his head with positiveness.

"I must have it recut," said he, "and by the best man obtainable."

"Ah, that is Van der Veen, the Hollander. He does all my important work. But Van der Veen will himself argue against the desecration. He is a man of judgment."

"Where can I find him?" asked the prince.

The merchant reflected.

"I will give you a letter to him," said he. "If the stone must be recut, I want Van der Veen to do it himself. He has three sons who are all expert workmen, but no one in the world can excel the father."

He wrote the note, addressed it, and gave it to Kāra. Then he again picked up the ruby and examined it.

"If you would but sell it," he suggested, with hesitation, "I could secure for you a liberal price. The Khedive has placed with me an order for a necklace of the ancient Egyptian gems; but in two years I have been unable to secure more than three stones, none of which compare with this in size or beauty. Allow me."

He opened a drawer and displayed the three antique stones—two emeralds and an amethyst. Kāra smiled, and putting his hand in a pocket underneath his burnous, he drew out five more rubies, but little inferior in size to the one he had first shown.

"Tell me," said he, "what price you will pay for these, to add to the Khedive's necklace."

Andalaft was amazed, but concealed his joy and eagerness as much as possible. Carefully he examined the gems under a glass and then weighed each one in his scales.

"I will give you," said he, after figuring a little, "four hundred pounds for the five stones."

Kāra shrugged his shoulders and picked up the rubies.

"That may be the price for ordinary gems," he remarked; "but their age and cutting give these an added value. I am holding them at eight hundred pounds."

The merchant smiled.

"It is easy to understand," said he, with politeness, "that you are a connoisseur of precious stones; but, because you love the antique, your partiality induces you to place an undue value upon your rubies. Come! let us say six hundred."

"I will not bargain," returned the Egyptian; "nor do I urge you to buy. If you cannot afford to pay my price I will keep the rubies," and he made a motion to gather them up.

"Stay!" exclaimed the jeweler. "What does it matter? The Khedive wishes them, and I must make the sacrifice for his pleasure."

With a hand he vainly endeavored to render steady he wrote a check for the sum demanded, and Kāra took it and went away. Andalaft had made an excellent bargain; yet the Egyptian, for all his cleverness, did not know that he had been victimized.

At the house of the diamond-cutter, on a quiet side street at the lower end of the Mouski, Kāra had a long interview with Van der Veen and his three sons. As a result they agreed, after examining the magnificent diamonds shown them, to devote their exclusive services to Prince Kāra for a full year, he promising to keep them busy with the work of recutting his collection of ancient gems.

Afterward he sent Tadros with notes to Gerald Winston and the banker, informing them of his temporary address, as he had promised. Then he had an excellent luncheon and smoked a Cuban cigar. In the afternoon he followed his imploring dragoman into several shops where he made simple purchases, and returned early to his hotel to find Winston impatiently awaiting him.

"You must accompany me at once to see my friend Professor Daressy, with whom I am already disputing concerning the new papyri. He is much interested in your method of interpreting the manuscripts, but requires a better proof of its accuracy than I can give him. Will you come?"

"It will give me pleasure," answered Kāra—he drove with Winston to the curator's house. His knowledge of the hieroglyphics was well founded, and he was not averse to an argument with the two savants.

Indeed, they found his explanations so clear and concise that they were equally amazed and delighted.

The Egyptian dined with them in a private room, where the discussion could not be interrupted, and it was late in the evening when he returned thoughtfully to his own humble lodging.

"Tadros," said he, "find me a comfortable house in a good part of the city. Something like that of Professor Daressy will do."

"It will cost a lot of money," objected the dragoman.

"Never mind; I will pay the price," returned the prince, haughtily.

So the next day Tadros rented a furnished house near the Ezbekieh Gardens for twelve hundred piastres a month, and charged Kāra two thousand piastres for it. The prince moved in, and for three or four weeks devoted himself to watching the Van der Veens recut his treasures, to long conversations with those Egyptologists who were spending the heated term in Cairo, and to a study of the collection of ancient relics in the great museum which Maspero had founded under Said Pasha. Incidentally he observed the social life and manners of those with whom he came in contact, and acquired a polish of his own in a surprisingly short period.

At the end of the month he returned to Fedah, taking his dragoman with him. Tadros went without protest, for he was making excellent profits from his old-time friend and had perfected a system of robbery that almost doubled Prince Kāra's expenses.

They traveled by train and crossed the river in a boat, arriving in the evening at the tiny village. Tadros carried Kāra's large traveling case and walked behind him, as was fitting in a paid retainer.

And so they entered the narrow street of the village, where all the dozen or so inhabitants stood in their doorways to stare and nod gravely at their returned fellow-citizens.

Kāra bade his dragoman leave the luggage in his own dwelling and seek a lodging for himself with old Nefert or Amenka. He then walked on to where Sĕra and her daughter awaited him.

He pinched Nephthys' fat cheeks, felt of her round bare arms, and finally kissed her lips, declaring that she was steadily improving in condition and would put to shame many of the women of Cairo.

Nephthys allowed the caresses listlessly, her eyes only brightening slightly when the gaily dressed dragoman came near and stood watching the proceedings. He wore a green jacket with gold embroidery today, and the girl observed it with evident approval.

"I sold her too cheaply, Kāra," remarked the dragoman, stroking his thin mustache reflectively.

"In that I do not agree with you," answered Kāra.

"I will pay double the price for her return," said Tadros.

"The girl is not for sale. And see here, my man, keep your hands off her while you are in Fedah, or I will be obliged to kill you."

"Never fear; I know my duties," replied the dragoman, turning on his heel. It would not be wise to offend Kāra just now. The bone was not yet picked.

Nephthys put on her spangled gown and sat upon Kāra's knee, while her mother brought cakes and milk for their refreshment. Kāra threw a chain of beads over the girl's head, and she laughed for very pleasure. Sĕra felt of the beads and counted them. They were blue, and had cost five piastres, but the two women were delighted with them and would enjoy their possession for many days.

It was late when Kāra left Sĕra's hut.

"In the winter," said he, "I will doubtless come for the girl and take her to Cairo. Then you shall have the rest of your money. Meantime, here is backshish to console you."

He gave her a piece of gold—the first she had ever possessed—and went away to his dwelling.

"Nephthys," said the mother, "I am proud of you. You have made us both rich!"

VIII

His Grandmother's Mummy

When Fedah seemed asleep, Kāra took the lamp and the bronze dagger from their hiding place and swung back the stone in the rear wall, passing through into the mountain cavern. Then, replacing the stone, he made his way along the crevice, through the circular rock door into the arched passage, and down the latter to the mummy chamber.

Here he removed the lid of Hatatcha's mummy case and carefully dusted the interior. The forty days were ended. The case might have its occupant before morning.

Within the splendidly carven casket Kāra found an oblong green stone, with polished flat surfaces. On one of these surfaces was the cartouche of Ahtka-Rā, as follows:

The Egyptian examined this relic carefully and placed it in his pocket. It was the emerald that Hatatcha had promised the dwarf Sebbet in payment for embalming her body. How Andalaft's eyes would sparkle could he but see this wonder!

But this thought reminded Kāra that he was loitering. He picked up his lamp and went to the mummy of Ahtka-Rā, sliding back the slab of malachite and descending through the opening to the treasure chamber hidden below.

His first act was to inventory carefully the contents of the twelve great vases that stood upon their alabaster pedestals. From these vases he abstracted choice specimens of emeralds, sapphires, diamonds and rubies, filling with them several small leathern sacks he had brought concealed upon his person. Perhaps he had taken a fortune in this careless manner; but so vast was the treasure that the contents of the vases seemed scarcely disturbed.

In one of the numerous jars resting upon the granite floor, and which had doubtless been added to the hoard at a much later period than that of Ahtka-Rā, the Egyptian found a quantity of pearls of a size and quality that rendered them almost peerless among the treasures of the world. The jar contained a full quart, and Kāra took them all. At the moment he did not comprehend their value, although Hatatcha had told him that a single one of these pearls would be sufficient to ransom a kingdom.

The gems he had already secured were enough to weigh heavily upon his person; but Kāra was greedy. He examined the contents of many jars and vases, choosing here and there a jewel that appealed to his fancy, and adding to his selection a number of exquisite ornaments of wrought gold; but at last he was forced to admit that he had taken enough from the treasure chamber to answer his present purposes, and so he reluctantly returned to the vault above.

As he closed the slab, his eye fell upon a strange jewel set in the mummy case of Ahtka-Rā. It was surrounded by a protecting band of chased gold, and sparkled under the rays of Kāra's lamp in a manner that distinguished it from any of the thousands of other gems that literally covered the mummy case of the great Egyptian; for at first this odd jewel had a dark steely lustre, which changed while Kāra's eyes rested upon it to a rich transparent orange, and then to an opal ground with tongues of flame running through it. A moment later the color had faded to a dull gray, which gradually took on a greenish tinge.

Kāra set down the lamp and pried the stone from its setting with the point of his dagger, placing it afterward in a secure inner pocket of his robe. As he did so, a golden bust of Isis that stood upon the mummy case toppled and fell to the pavement, and from a hollow underneath the bust rolled a small manuscript of papyrus. This Kāra took also, and replaced the bust in its former position. His nerves must have been of iron, for the uncanny incident had not even startled him.

Now he made his way back to the entrance and along the passage, finally emerging with his treasure into the room that had been his former dwelling-place. All was silent and dark. A mild bray from the blind Nikko's donkey was occasionally heard, and at times the far-away hoot of a desert owl; but those within the village seemed steeped in slumber.

Kāra divided his burden by placing the greater part in his traveling case, which he locked securely. Then he reclined upon the rushes and was about to compose himself to sleep when the mat across the archway was thrust aside and Sebbet entered.

"I am here, most royal one!" he announced.

Kāra sat up.

"And my grandmother?" he inquired.

"Here also, my prince. Ah, how natural is Hatatcha! You will be

L. FRANK BAUM

delighted. It is a skilful and almost perfect piece of work, even though I praise my own craft in saying so."

With these words the dwarf led in the donkey. Upon its back was the form of a swaddled mummy, which was bound to a flat plank to hold it rigidly extended.

"I will show you the face," continued Sebbet, in an eager tone, as he lifted the mummy and placed it upon the ground.

"Do not trouble yourself," said Kāra. "I will look upon my grandmother at my leisure. The night is waning. Take your price and go your way."

He handed the dwarf the emerald, holding the lamp, which he had relighted, while Sebbet examined the stone with great care.

"Yes; it is the great emerald with the cartouche of Ahtka-Rā," said the embalmer, in a low, grave voice. "Osiris be praised that at last it is my own! Hatatcha was a wise woman, and she kept her word."

Kāra extinguished the light, but the moon was shining and sent some of its rays through the arch to relieve the gloom.

"Goodnight," said he.

The dwarf stood still, thinking deeply. Finally he said, glancing at the mummy:

"Where will my old friend repose?"

"It is her secret," returned the prince, brusquely. "She trusted you not to ask questions."

"And yourself? Will you not wish to be mummified when your course is run?"

Kāra laughed.

"Ah, my Sebbet, are you immortal?" he asked. "Do you expect to live to embalm all the generations? You made a mummy of my great-grandmother and of my grandmother. Your hairs are now white. Be content, and think upon your own future."

"That has already occupied my mind," answered the dwarf, quietly. "Farewell, then, prince of a royal line. Your ancestors thought first of the tomb, then of the life preceding it. You are indulging in life, with no thought of the tomb and the resurrection. It is the new order of things, the trend of a civilization that forgets its dead and hides the silent ones in the earth, that they may putrify and decay and become mere dust. Very well; the age is yours, not mine. May Osiris guide thy life, my prince!"

He turned to his donkey and led the ghost-like animal out into the night. Kāra stood still, and in a moment he could hear their footsteps no longer.

Then he secured the mat before the arch and for a second time swung back the stone in the wall. This done, he felt in the dusk for the mummy of Hatatcha, and lifting it in his arms, bore it through the opening and replaced the stone. The body was heavy, and he panted as he paused to light his lamp.

It was nearly an hour before Kāra, weary and perspiring, finally deposited the mummy of his grandmother beside its elaborately constructed case. He then unfastened the straps that bound it to the board, and by exercising great care succeeded in placing the body in its coffin without breaking or injuring it. Next he removed the outer strips of linen that swathed the head until the outlines of Hatatcha's face showed clearly through its mask of tightly drawn bandages. Then he stood aside, and holding up the lamp, gazed long and earnestly upon the calm features.

"I promised," he murmured, "here to repeat my oath: That I will show no mercy to anyone of Lord Roane's family; that I will hunt them down, everyone, as a tiger hunts his prey, and crush and humble them in the eyes of all men; that not one shall finally escape my vengeance, and that all shall know in the end that it was Hatatcha who destroyed them. So be it. By Āmen-Rā, the Sun-God who gave me being; by Ahtka-Rā, whose blood now courses through my veins; by my hope of peace on earth and in the life to come, I swear that Hatatcha's will shall be obeyed!"

His voice was cold and even of tone; his face grave, but unmoved. He placed his hand upon the breast of the mummy and repeated the mystic sign he had used at her death-bed. This done, he raised the heavy carved lid of the case and placed it in position.

Next morning Kāra gave Nephthys a kiss and returned across the river on his way to Cairo. The dragoman carried the traveling bag and grumbled at its weight. He was in a bad humor. It is all very well to make money, and Kāra is a veritable mine; but had Tadros realized that Nephthys was so fat and flabby, it would have required much more than a roll of papyrus to induce him to part with her. True, he had managed, while her master was asleep, to stealthily meet the girl and embrace her; but he lacked the satisfaction that exists in proprietorship. One should be careful about selling young women. They are like untried camels—liable to develop unexpected and valuable qualities.

These reflections engrossed the dragoman all the way to Cairo; but there were other things to demand his attention. Prince Kāra announced his intention of taking the next steamer to Naples, and then traveling to Paris and London. He asked Tadros to accompany him.

"But that is impossible!" was the reply. "I am a dragoman of Egypt, the chief of my profession, a guide unequaled for knowledge, intelligence and fidelity in all the land! But take me away from my own country, and what am I? Take me from the poor tourists, and what will become of them?"

"I need you in Europe, to do things in my service that I would not dare propose to anyone else. I believe," said the prince, coolly, "that you are an unprincipled scoundrel. You lie easily and without hesitation; you rob me cheerfully everyday that you are in my employ; you have no conscience and no morality, except that you are afraid of the law. I have studied your character with care, and I have estimated it aright."

Tadros first looked shame-faced, then humble, then indignant.

"By every god of Egypt," he cried, earnestly, "I am an honest man!"

"That is proof of my assertion to the contrary," replied the unmoved Kāra. "Now, I need a scoundrel to assist me, and you are the man of my choice. Continue to fleece me, if you like; I do not mind. But if you serve me faithfully in some delicate matters that will soon require my attention, I will make you the richest dragoman alive, so that Raschid and the Haieks will all turn green with envy. On the other hand, should you choose to betray me, you will not require riches, for the nether world has no commerce."

Tadros thought it over.

"We are Egyptians," he said, at last. "Your enemies are equally mine. Very well; command and I will obey. Are you not a prince of my people? And why should I ever wish to betray you?"

"Because wise men sometimes become fools. In your case a lapse from wisdom means death. Others may bribe you with an equal amount of money, but I alone will exact the penalty for betrayal. I think you will remain wise."

"Ah, that is certain, my prince!" declared Tadros, with conviction.

And so Kāra sailed from Alexandria, taking with him the great diamonds which the Van der Veens had already recut, the wonderful pearls which no eye but his had yet beheld, and the priceless treasures of Ahtka-Rā.

The dragoman followed him, humble and obedient.

IX

Aneth

Charles Consinor, ninth Earl of Roane, was considerably discouraged at the moment when Luke the butler placed the big blue government envelope upon his table, thoughtfully leaving it at the top of the daily heap of missives from impatient creditors.

During a gay and dissipated life, his lordship had seen the ample fortune left him by his father gradually melt away, until now, in his old age, he found it difficult to secure sufficient funds to enable him to maintain a respectable position in the world. He had been ably assisted in his extravagances by his only son, the Viscount Roger Consinor, who for twenty years past had performed his full share in dissipating the family fortunes.

Aside from their mutual prodigality, however, the two men had little in common. The father was reckless, open-handed and careless of consequences, indulging himself frankly in such dissipations as most men are careful to hide. The son was reserved and sullen, and posed as a man eminently respectable, confining his irregularities mainly to the gaming table. Between them they had loaded the estates with mortgages and sold every stick and stone that could be sold. At last the inevitable happened and they faced absolute ruin.

There seemed no way out of their difficulties. The viscount had unfortunately married a wife with no resources whatever, although her family connections were irreproachable. The poor viscountess had been a confirmed invalid ever since her baby girl was born, some eighteen years before, and was merely tolerated in the big, half-ruined London mansion, being neglected alike by her husband and her father-in-law, who had both come to look upon her as a useless incumbrance. More than that, they resented the presence of a young, awkward girl in the house, and for that reason banished Aneth at twelve to a girl's school in Cheshire, where she had remained, practically forgotten, until her eighteenth year. Then the lady preceptress shipped her home because her tuition fee was not promptly paid.

Aneth found her mother so confirmed in the selfish habits of the persistent invalid, that the girl's society, fresh and cheery though it proved, only irritated her nerves. She found her father, the morose viscount, absolutely indifferent and unresponsive to her desire to be loved and admitted into his companionship. But old Lord Roane, her grandfather, had still a weakness for a pretty face, and Aneth was certainly pretty. Moreover, she was sweet and pure and maidenly, and no one was better able to admire and appreciate such qualities than the worn-out roué whose life had been mainly spent in the society of light women. So he took the girl to his evil old heart, and loved her, and tried to prevent her discovering how unworthy he was of her affection. The love for his granddaughter became the one unselfish, honest love of his life, and it assisted wonderfully in restoring in him some portion of his long-lost self-respect.

Aneth, finding no other friend in the gloomy establishment that was now her home, soon became devoted, in turn, to her grandsire, and although she was shrewd enough, in spite of her inexperience, to realize that his life had been, and still was, somewhat coarse and dissipated, she fondly imagined that her influence would, to an extent, reclaim him—which it actually did, but only to an extent.

There was little concealment in the family circle as to the state of their finances. Father and son quarreled openly about the division of what little money could be raised on the overburdened estates, and the girl was not long in realizing the difficulties of their position. If the viscount had nothing to gamble with, he became insufferable and almost brutal in his manner; if Lord Roane could not afford to dine at the club and amuse himself afterward, he was irritable and abusive to all with whom he came in contact, save only his granddaughter. The household expenses were matters of credit, and the wages of the servants were greatly in arrears.

And so, when the affairs of the family had become well-nigh desperate, the big blue envelope with the government stamp arrived, and like magic all their difficulties dissolved.

A newly appointed cabinet minister—a man whom Lord Roane had reason to consider an enemy rather than a friend—had for some surprising and unknown reason interested himself in Roane's behalf, and the result was a diplomatic post for him in Egypt under Lord Cromer, and a position for the viscount in the Egyptian Department of Finance. The appointments were lucrative and honorable, and indicated the Government's perfect confidence in both father and son.

Lord Roane was astounded. Never would he have dared demand such consideration, and to have these honors thrust upon him at a time when they would practically rescue his name and fortune from ruin was almost unbelievable.

He accepted the appointment with alacrity, joyful at the prospect of a winter in gay Cairo. Roger shared his father's felicity, because the gaming in the oriental city would be more fascinating than that of London, where people had begun to frown when he entered a room. The invalid viscountess hoped Egypt would benefit her health. Aneth welcomed any change from the horrible condition in which they had existed latterly.

"Grandfather," said she, gravely, "our gracious Queen has given to you and to my father positions of great trust. I am sure that you will personally do your duty loyally, and with credit to our honored name; but I'm afraid for father. Will you promise me to keep him from card-playing and urge him to lead a more reputable life?"

"Phoo! Nonsense, child. Roger will behave himself, I am sure, now that he will have important duties to occupy him. The Minister of Finance will keep him busy, never fear, and he will have neither time nor inclination for folly. Don't worry, little one. Our fortunes have changed; we shall now be able to pay the butcher and baker and candlestick-maker, and there is little doubt the Consinors will speedily become the pride of the nation. Ahem! Tell Luke, my dear, to fetch my brandy and soda as you go out. And, stay! Remember, we are to leave London on the fourth of October and you must have both your mother and yourself ready to depart promptly. I depend upon you, Aneth."

She kissed him and went away without further comment, reflecting, with a sigh, that her fears and warnings were alike unheeded.

Lord Roane, left to himself, began wondering anew to what whim of fate he owed his good fortune. Really, there seemed no clue to the mystery.

It was a complicated matter, even to one on the inside, so it is no wonder the old nobleman failed to comprehend it.

Many years ago the cabinet minister and Lord Roane had been intimate friends; then the former fell madly in love with a little Egyptian princess who was the rage of the London season, and sought her hand in marriage. Roane also became enamored of the beautiful Hatatcha, and went so far as to apply for a divorce from his wife, that he might wed her. The fascinating Egyptian, guileless of European customs and won by the masterful ardor of Roane, chose him from among all her suitors, and casting aside the honest love of Roane's friend, fell unconsciously into the trap set for her and became the mistress of the man who promised her such rare devotion. Presently, however, the heartless roué tired of his easy conquest and carelessly thrust her aside, although the divorce for which he had applied on false representations had now been granted, and he was free to marry his victim had he so wished.

All London was indignant at his act at the time, and no one was more enraged than Roane's former friend. He searched everywhere for the Egyptian princess when Hatatcha fled from London to hide her shame, and on his return from the unsuccessful quest, he quarreled with Roane and would have killed him had not mutual friends interposed.

Time had, of course, seared all these old wounds, although the hatred between the two men would endure to the grave. The betrayer was careless of criticism and wealthy enough to defy it. The man who had truly loved was broken-hearted, and from that time avoided all society and especially that of women. But he plunged into politics for diversion, and in that field won for himself such honor and renown in future years that at last he became a member of Her Majesty's cabinet, second in power only to the Premier himself.

Thus Prince Kāra found him. The Egyptian had only to use the magic name of Hatatcha to secure a private audience with the great man, who listened quietly while Kāra demanded vengeance upon his grandmother's betrayer.

"In England," said the minister, "there is no vendetta. The rage I fostered thirty-odd years ago, when my heart was wrung with despair, has long since worn itself out. Time evens up these old scores without human interference. Roane is today on the verge of ruin. His only son is a confirmed gambler. Their race is nearly run, and the gray hairs of Hatatcha's false lover will go dishonored to the grave. Is that not enough?"

"By no means," returned Prince Kāra, with composure. "They must be made to suffer as my grandmother suffered, but with added agony for the years of impunity that have elapsed. It was her will—the desire of her long, miserable life. Will you, her old friend, deny her right to be avenged?"

A flood of resentment swept into the heart of the listener. Years may sear a wound; but if it is deep, the scar remains.

"What do you ask of me?" he answered.

Before replying, Kāra reflected for sometime, his eyes steadily fixed upon the floor.

"Are there no women in Lord Roane's family?" he asked, finally.

"There are two, I believe—his son's wife, who is an invalid, and his granddaughter."

"Ah!" The long-drawn exclamation was one of triumphant satisfaction. Again the Egyptian relapsed into thought, and the minister was growing impatient when his strange visitor at last spoke.

"Sir," said he, "you ask me what you can do to assist me. I will tell you. Obtain for Lord Roane a diplomatic post in Cairo, under Lord Cromer. Obtain some honorable place for his son as well. That will take the entire family to Egypt—my own country."

"Well?"

"In London there is no vendetta. Crimes that the law cannot reach are allowed to go unpunished. In Egypt we are Nature's children. No false civilization glosses our wrongs or denies our right to protect our honor. I implore you, my lord, as you respect the memory of poor Hatatcha, to send Lord Roane and his family to Egypt."

"I will," said the minister, with stern brow.

And so it was that the Government remembered old Lord Roane, and likewise his illustrious son, the Viscount Roger Consinor, and sent them to Egypt on missions of trust.

X

LORD CROMER'S RECEPTION

It was but natural that Lord Cromer, with his intense loyalty to the home Government, should endeavor to show every honor to the latest recipients of Her Majesty's favor. He gave a splendid dinner to Lord Roane and his family, which was followed by a reception attended by nearly every important personage then in Cairo.

At the dinner Gerald Winston was introduced to Aneth Consinor, and had the good fortune to be selected to escort her to the table. She won the big Englishman with the first glance from her clear, innocent eyes, and he was delighted to find that she conversed easily and with intelligence upon the themes that most interested him.

Winston knew something of the reputation of Lord Roane at home, and remembered not only his intrigue with the Egyptian princess in his youth, but the gossip of many more recent escapades that were distinctly unsavory. He had also heard whispers concerning his son, the viscount, that served to cast more or less discredit upon a name already sadly tarnished; but no one could look into Aneth's candid eyes without being convinced that she was innocent of the sins of her fathers. Winston exonerated her at once of any possible contamination from such sources, rejoicing exultantly that the English maiden was unconscious of the smirch of her environments. However, as he listened to the girl's bright chatter, an incongruous thought struck him and made him frown involuntarily. He remembered that she was a cousin—on the left hand, to be sure, but no less an unrecognized second cousin—to that dirty Egyptian whom he had lately discovered under the palms of Fedah, and who had since, by an astonishing evolution, become Prince Kāra. Lord Roane was grandfather to them both. It was not Aneth's fault—perhaps she would never know of the illicit relationship; but his own knowledge of the fact rendered him uneasy for her sake, and he began to wish she had never been allowed to set foot in Egypt.

But here she was, and apparently very happy and contented by his side.

"Perhaps I am wrong in my estimate of Cleopatra," she was saying; "but the inscriptions on the temple at Dendera seem to prove her to have been religious and high-minded to a degree. Perhaps it is Shakespeare's romance of Antony and Cleopatra that has poisoned our minds as to the character of a noble woman."

"Have you been to Dendera?" he asked; "and can you read the inscriptions?"

"I have penetrated into Egypt no farther than Cairo, Mr. Winston," she responded, with a laugh; "therefore my acquaintance with the temples is confined to what I have read. But at my school was a teacher passionately fond of Egyptology, and around her she gathered a group of girls whom she inspired with a similar love for the subject. We have read everything we could procure that might assist us in our studies, and—don't laugh, sir!—I can even write hieroglyphics a bit myself."

"That is quite simple," said he, smiling; "but can you decipher and translate the sign language?"

"No; so many individual signs mean so many different things, and it is so impossible to decide whether the inscription begins to read from right to left, or in the middle, or up or down!"

"That may well puzzle more experienced heads than yours, Miss Consinor," said he. "Indeed, I know of but one man living who reads the hieroglyphics unerringly."

"And who is that?" she asked, with eager interest.

He bit his lip, blaming himself for the thoughtless slip of his tongue. Nothing should induce him to mention Kāra by name to this girl.

"A native whom I recently met," he answered, evasively. "But tell me, are you not going to make the Nile trip?"

"I hope so, when my grandfather has time to take me; but he says his new duties will require all his present attention, and unfortunately they are connected with the new works in the Delta rather than with upper Egypt." She glanced across at Lord Roane, who was conversing lightly with two high dignitaries, and his eyes followed hers. "But won't you tell me something of your own experiences in the Nile country?" she asked. "I am told you are a very great discoverer, and have lately unearthed a number of priceless ancient papyri."

"They are interesting," returned Winston, modestly, "but not so extraordinary as to deserve your comment. Indeed, Miss Consinor, although I have been many years in Egypt, engaged in quiet explorations, I cannot claim to have added much to the vast treasures that have been accumulated."

"But His Grace the Khedive has made you a Bey," she persisted.

He laughed frankly and without affectation.

"The Khedive has this cheerful way of rewarding those who will spend their money to make his ancient domain famous," he replied. "Beys are as plentiful in Egypt as are counts in France."

"But you have made *some* discoveries, I am sure. The wonderful papyri, for instance—where did you find them?"

"I bought them, Miss Consinor, with good English money."

She appeared disappointed, but brightened a moment later.

"At least it was you who discovered and excavated the birth-house at Kom Ombos. I have read your article concerning it in the *Saturday Review*."

"Then you know all about it," said he. "But see; nearly opposite us is the great Maspero himself—the man who has done more for Egypt than all the rest of us combined. Does he not look the savant? Let me tell you something of his most important work."

Here was a subject he could talk on fluently and with fervor, and she listened as attentively as he could desire.

After dinner they repaired to the great hall of the palace, to participate in the reception. Lord Cromer was soon gracefully greeting his guests and presenting them to Lord Roane, Viscount Consinor and the Honorable Aneth Consinor.

Gerald Winston, standing at a distance from the group, gave an involuntary shiver as he saw Prince Kāra brought forward and presented.

Lord Roane greeted the Egyptian with the same cordiality he had bestowed uniformly upon his host's other guests. Why should he not? Only Winston, silently observant in the background, knew their relationship—except Kāra. Yes; Kāra knew, for he had said so that day beneath the palms of Fedah. But now his demeanor was grave and courteous, and his countenance composed and inscrutable.

Aneth smiled upon the handsome native as he passed slowly on to give place to others.

Kāra, who now affected European dress, wore the conventional evening costume; but he was distinguished by the massive and curious chain that hung from his neck, as well as by a unique gem that he wore upon a finger of his left hand. It had no real color, yet it attracted every eye as surely as if it possessed a subtle magnetism that was irresistible. No one saw it in the same aspect, for one declared it blue, another gray, a third brown and the next one green. But all agreed that it had a strange, fascinating gleam, and declared that it radiated tiny tongues of flame.

It was the stone Kāra had picked from the burial case of Ahtka-Rā.

Later in the evening the Egyptian found opportunity for a short conversation with Aneth, who was plainly attracted by this distinguished-appearing native. He found her curious concerning the chain of the kings, and proudly explained it to her, reading some of the inscriptions upon the links.

"Sometime," said he, "it will give me pleasure to go over all the links with you, for in them is condensed the history of the great kings of the early dynasties. There is not another such record in existence."

"I can well believe it," replied the girl. "You must honor me with a call, Prince Kāra, for I am an ardent Egyptologist, although a very ignorant one."

"I thank you," said Kāra, bowing low; "I shall esteem it a privilege to enlighten you so far as I am able. My country has a wonderful history, and much of it is not yet printed in books."

Shortly after this he left the reception, although many of the ladies would have been delighted to lionize him. He had become known in the capital as the last of the descendants of the ancient kings of Egypt; and while more than one was skeptical of the truth of this statement, its corroboration by the natives who knew of his lineage, the wide advertisement given his claims by Tadros, the dragoman, and the enormous wealth the Prince was reputed to possess, all contributed to render him a most interesting figure in Cairoene society. It is certain that had he cared to remain at Lord Cromer's reception, he would have met with no lack of attention; but his object in attending was now accomplished, and he left the assemblage and found his carriage awaiting him in the driveway.

"Home!" said he, in Coptic, and his dragoman nodded cheerfully and sprang upon the box. The journey was made in moody silence.

Meantime Winston rejoined Aneth and found her a seat in a quiet corner, where they could converse undisturbed. He had watched Kāra uneasily while the Egyptian was addressing the English girl, and now inwardly resolved to counteract any favorable impression the native prince might have made upon her unsophisticated mind.

Why he should interest himself so strangely in this young woman he could not have explained. Many a fair maid had smiled upon Gerald Winston without causing his heart to beat one jot the faster. Nay, they had at times even practiced their arts to win him, for the bluff, good-looking young Englishman was wealthy enough to be regarded a good catch. But the society of fashionable ladies was sure to weary him in time, and here in Egypt he met only butterflies from England and America, or the coarse-featured, stolid native women, who had no power to interest any European of intelligence.

But Aneth Consinor seemed different from all the others. Not because she was fresh and sweet and girlish, for he had seen nice girls before; not that she was beautiful, because many women possess that enviable gift; not that she was gracious and intelligent, with a fascinating charm of manner, although that counts for much in winning men's hearts. Perhaps, after all, it was her sincerity and the lights that lay in the clear depths of her wonderful eyes that formed her chief attraction. The eyes, he remembered, had impressed him at first, and they were destined to retain their power over him to the last.

And the strangest thing of all, it occurred to him, as he sat pleasantly chatting with her, was the fact that she was Lord Roane's granddaughter and the child of Lord Consinor. A remark that Kāra had once made flashed across his mind: "The father, giving so little to his progeny, can scarce contaminate it, whatever he may chance to be." Perhaps this was more logical than he had hitherto cared to believe.

Aneth mentioned Prince Kāra presently, and asked whether he knew him.

"Yes," he answered; "it was I who discovered him. Kāra is one of my few finds."

"And where was he discovered?" she asked, amused at his tone.

"In a mud village on the Nile bank, clothed in rags and coated with dirt. But he was very intelligent, for he had been educated by a clever relative who had once lived in the world; and, in some way, he and his people had access to an ancient hoarded treasure, so that the man was rich without knowing how to utilize his wealth. I purchased his treasure—or a part of it, at least—and brought him to Cairo. He was observant and quick to adapt himself to his new surroundings. He sold more treasure, I have since learned, and visited Paris and London. In six months the dirty Nile dweller has become a man of the world, and society accepted him because he is rich and talented."

"How curious!" she exclaimed. "And is he, indeed, a descendant of the ancient kings?"

"So I believe—on his mother's side, for the Egyptians trace their descent only from their mothers. Yet they are so inconsistent that it is of their fathers they boast. The Egyptian women have usually been poor creatures, listless and unintelligent. In this they differ from the women of almost every other semi-tropical country."

"They must have been different in the olden times," said the girl, gravely; "for it is not likely that the first real civilization of the world sprang from a stupid race. And think for how many centuries these poor creatures have been enslaved and trodden into the dust. I am inclined to think the contempt with which the Saracens regarded women is responsible for their present condition in Egypt. Have you found none of them clever or womanly, as we understand the latter term?"

He thought of Hatatcha.

"There are doubtless a few exceptions, even in these days," he answered. "And you are right about ancient women having had their place in Egyptian history. Besides poor Cleopatra, whom you so bravely defended at dinner, there was Queen Hatasu, you know; and Nitocris, Hatshepset and others who rendered themselves immortal. Have you visited our museum yet?"

"Only for a glance around; but that glance was enough to fill me with awe and wonder. I mean to devote many days to the study of its treasures."

"Let me go with you," he begged. "It would please me to watch your eager enjoyment of the things I know so well. And I can help you a little."

"You are very good, indeed," said the girl, delighted at the suggestion. "We will go tomorrow afternoon, if you can spare the time."

"May I call for you?" he asked.

"If you please. I will be ready at one o'clock, for I must take full advantage of my opportunity."

So he went home filled with elation at the promise of tomorrow. And never before had Gerald Winston given a thought to a woman after leaving her presence.

Tonight he dreamed, and the dream was of Aneth.

XI

SETTING THE SNARES

Kāra also dreamed. The girl's eyes haunted him. He saw her bright, eager glance, her appealing smile, the graceful pose of her beautiful head wherever he might chance to look. And he cursed the persistent vision and tried to exorcise it, well knowing it might lead to his undoing.

The Egyptian's present establishment consisted of a handsome villa on the Shubra road which at one time had been owned by a high Turkish official. It was splendidly furnished, including many modern conveniences, and had a pretty garden in the court that led from the master's quarters to the harem. Tadros, the dragoman, proudly boasted to himself—he dared not confide in others—that the furnishing of this villa had enabled him to acquire a snug fortune. Kāra allowed him a free hand, and much gold refused to pass through the dragoman's fingers.

Tadros had ceased to bemoan the loss of his beloved tourists by this time. Even a dozen profligate Americans could not enrich him as his own countryman was doing. And the end was not yet.

A few days after the reception Kāra lunched at the Lotus Club and met there Lord Consinor. Later the prince played a game of écarté with Colonel Varrin, of the Khedivial army, and lost a large sum. Consinor watched the game with interest, and after the colonel had retired proposed to take a hand with the Egyptian himself. To this Kāra politely assented. He was a careless player, and displayed little judgment. The result was that he lost again, and Consinor found himself the richer by a hundred pounds.

The prince laughed good-humoredly and apologized for his poor playing.

"The next time you favor me with a game," said he, "I will try to do better."

Consinor smiled grimly. To meet so wealthy and indifferent a victim was indeed rare good luck. He promised himself to fleece the inexperienced Egyptian with exceptional pleasure.

The Lotus Club was then, as now, the daily resort of the most prominent and at the same time the fastest set in Cairo. Both Roane and Consinor had been posted for membership, although the former seldom visited the place until after midnight, and then only to sup or indulge in a bottle of wine when there was nothing more amusing to do. It appeared that Lord Roane was conducting himself with exceptional caution since his arrival in Cairo. His official duties were light, and he passed most of his days at the rooms in the Savoy, where his party was temporarily located until a suitable house could be secured and fitted up. He left Aneth much alone in the evenings, however, and the girl was forced to content herself with the gaieties of the fashionable hotel life and the companionship of those few acquaintances who called upon her. As for the viscount, he was now, as always, quite outside the family circle, and while he seemed attentive to his desk at the Department of Finance, the office hours were over at midday and he was free to pass the afternoons and evenings at the club. The viscountess remained languidly helpless and clung to her own apartment, where she kept a couple of Arab servants busy waiting upon her.

Consinor had told Aneth that he would not touch a card while he remained in Egypt; but if he had ever had an idea of keeping his word the resolution soon vanished. He found Kāra irresistible. Sometimes, to be sure, the prince had luck and won, but in that event it was his custom to double the stakes indefinitely until his opponent swept all his winnings away.

This reckless policy at first alarmed Consinor, who was accustomed to the cautious play of the London clubs; but he observed that Kāra declined ever to rise from the table a winner. No matter with whom he played, his opponent was sure to profit in the end by the Egyptian's peculiar methods. For this reason no man was more popular at the club or more eagerly sought as a partner in "a quiet game" than Prince Kāra, whose wealth seemed enormous and inexhaustible and whose generosity was proverbial.

But the rich Egyptian seemed to fancy Consinor's society above all other, and soon it came to be understood by the club's habitués that the two men preferred to play together, and the viscount was universally envied as a most fortunate individual.

Yet Kāra was occupying himself in other ways than card-playing during the weeks that followed the arrival of Lord Roane's party in Egypt. The victims of Hatatcha's hatred had been delivered into his net, and it was now necessary to spin his web so tightly about them that there could be no means of escape. The oriental mind is intricate. It seldom leads directly to a desired object or accomplishment, but prefers to plot cunningly and with involute complexity.

One of Lord Roane's few responsibilities was to audit the claims against the Egyptian Government of certain British contractors who were engaged in repairing the Rosetta Barrage and the canals leading from it. This barrage had originally been built in 1842, but was so badly done that important repairs had long been necessary. At one place a contractor named McFarland had agreed to build a stone embankment for two miles along the edge of a canal, to protect the country when the sluice-gates of the dam were opened. This man found, when he began excavating, that at one time a stone embankment had actually been built in this same place, although not high enough to be effective, for which reason it had become covered with Nile mud and its very existence forgotten. Finding that more than half of the work he had contracted to perform was already accomplished, the astute McFarland kept his lucky discovery a secret and proceeded to complete the embankment. Then he presented his bill for the entire work to be audited by Roane, after which he intended to collect from the Government. The matter involved the theft of eighteen thousand pounds sterling.

Kāra, whose well-paid spies were watching every official act of Lord Roane, learned of the contractor's plot by means of its betrayal to one of his men by McFarland himself, who, in an unguarded moment, when he was under the influence of drink, confided his good fortune to "his dear friend." But it was evident that Roane had no suspicion of the imposture and was likely to approve the fulfilment of the contract without hesitation.

Here was just the opportunity that the Egyptian had been seeking. One morning Tadros, being fully instructed, obtained a private interview with Lord Roane and confided to him his discovery of the clever plan of robbing the Government which McFarland was contemplating. Roane was surprised, but thanked the informer and promised to expose the swindle.

"That, my lord, would be a foolish thing to do," asserted the dragoman, bluntly. "The Egyptian Government is getting rich, and has ample money to pay for this contract and a dozen like it. I assure you that no one is aware of this secret but ourselves. Very well! Are we fools, my lord? Are there no commissions to be exacted to repay you for living in this country of the Turks, or me for keeping my ears open? I do not want your thanks; I want money. For a thousand pounds I will keep silent forever. For the rest, you can arrange your own division with the contractor."

Roane grew angry and indignant at once, asserting the dignity of his high office and blustering and threatening the dragoman for daring to so insult him. Tadros, however, was unimpressed.

"It is a mere matter of business," he suggested, when he was again allowed to proceed. "I am myself an Egyptian, but the Egyptians do not rule Egypt. Nor do I believe the English are here from entirely unselfish motives. To be frank, why should you or I endeavor to protect the stupid Turks, who are being robbed right and left? In this affair there is no risk at all, for if McFarland's dishonesty is discovered no one can properly accuse you of knowing the truth about the old embankment. Your inspector has gone there now; on his return he will say that the work is completed according to contract. You will approve the bill, McFarland will be paid, and I will then call upon you to collect my thousand pounds. Of your agreement with the contractor I wish to know nothing; so, then, the matter is settled. You can trust to my discretion, my lord."

Then he went away, leaving Roane to consider the proposition.

The old nobleman's career was punctured with such irregularities that the contemplation of this innocent-looking affair was in no way appalling to his moral sense. He merely pondered its safety, and decided the risk of exposure was small. Cairo was an extravagant city to live in, and his salary was too small to permit him to indulge in all the amusements he craved. The opportunity to acquire a snug amount was not to be despised, and, after all, the dragoman was correct in saying it would be folly not to take advantage of it.

The next day Kāra personally interviewed the contractor, telling him frankly that he was aware of all the details of the proposed swindle. McFarland was frightened, and protested that he had no intention of collecting the bill he had presented.

But the prince speedily reassured him.

"You must follow out your plans," said he. "It is too late to withdraw now. When you go to Roane he will inform you that he has discovered the truth. You will then compromise with him, offering him one-half of the entire sum you intend to steal, or a matter of nine thousand pounds. Give him more, if necessary; but remember that every piastre you allow Roane I will repay to you personally, if you can get my lord to sign a receipt to place in my hands."

"I see," said McFarland, nodding wisely. "You want to get him in your power."

"Precisely; and I am willing to pay well to do so."

"But when you expose him you will also implicate me."

"I shall not expose him. It will merely be a weapon for me to hold over him, but one I shall never use. You can depend upon that. Take your eighteen thousand pounds and go to England, where it will enable you to live in peace and affluence."

"I will," said the contractor. "I'll take the chances."

"There are none," returned Kāra, positively.

So it was that Lord Roane bargained successfully with the contractor and won for himself twelve of the eighteen thousand pounds for auditing the bill. The money was promptly paid by the Government and the division of spoils followed. Tadros called for his thousand pounds and gave a receipt for it that would incriminate himself if he ever dared divulge the secret. Roane also gave a receipt to McFarland, although reluctantly, and only when he found the matter could be arranged in no other way.

This receipt passed into the hands of Kāra. The contractor at once returned to England, and my lord secretly congratulated himself upon his "good luck" and began to enjoy his money.

While this little comedy was being enacted, Kāra found opportunity to call more than once upon Miss Aneth Consinor, who was charmed by his graceful speech and his exceptional knowledge of Egyptian history. Even Winston, whom Kāra met sometimes in the young lady's reception-room, could not deny the prince's claim to superior information concerning the ancients, and he listened as eagerly as Aneth to the man's interesting conversations, while impotently resenting the Egyptian's attention to the girl.

Aneth, however, knowing no reason why she should not admire the handsome native, whose personal attractions were by no means small, loved to draw him into discussions on his favorite themes and watch his dark, glowing eyes light up as he explained the mysteries of the priestly rites of the early dynasties. Whatever might be the man's secret designs, he always treated the English girl with rare gentleness and courtesy, although the bluntness of his speech and the occasional indelicacy of his allusions betrayed the crudeness of his early training. Winston grew to dislike and even to fear Kāra; for while he had nothing tangible with which to reproach the Egyptian, his experience of the native character led him to distrust the man intuitively.

Kāra doubtless felt this mistrust, for a coolness grew up between the two men that quickly destroyed their former friendship, and they soon came to mutually understand that they were rivals for Aneth's favor, and perhaps her affections.

Neither, however, had any idea of withdrawing from the field, and Aneth distributed her favors equally between them because she had no thought beyond her enjoyment of the society of the two men who had proved so especially agreeable. The girl had no chaperone except a young English lady whose rooms adjoined her own and with whom she had established a friendship; but Mrs. Everingham took a warm interest in the lonely girl and was glad to accompany her in many an excursion from which Aneth would otherwise have been debarred. The visits to the museum with Winston were frequent and of absorbing interest, for the handsome young Egyptologist was a delightful guide. Following an afternoon examining the famous relics, they would repair to the terrace at Shepheard's for five-o'clock tea, and here Kāra frequently joined them. The prince had brought from Paris an automobile, together with a competent French chauffeur, and in this machine many pleasant excursions were made to the pyramids, Heliopolis, Sakkara and Helwan, the Egyptian roads being almost perfection. Winston and Mrs. Everingham always joined these parties, and neither could fail to admit that Kāra was a delightful host.

XII

Nephthys

Kāra's plans were now maturing excellently, save in one particular. He did not wish to acquire a fondness for the girl who was his proposed victim, yet from the first she had cast a powerful spell over him, which all his secret struggles failed to remove. Waking or sleeping, her face was always before him, nor could he banish it even when engaged in play with her father at the club.

The Egyptian was shrewd enough to recognize danger in this extraordinary condition, and it caused him much uneasiness.

Finally, during a wakeful night, he thought of a means of escape.

"Tadros," said he to his dragoman in the morning, "go to Fedah and fetch Nephthys here. I have an empty harem at present; she shall be its first occupant."

Even the dragoman was surprised. He had begun to look upon his master as one affecting the manners and customs of the Europeans rather than the followers of the lax Muslim faith; but his face showed his pleasure at receiving the command.

"Most certainly, my prince," said he, with alacrity. "I will take the first train to Fedah, and the beauty shall be in your harem within three days."

Kāra caught the tone and the look.

"On second thought, Tadros," he said, gravely, "I will send Ebbek in your place. I may need your services here in Cairo."

"Ebbek! that doddering old Arab! He will never do at all," cried the dragoman, blusteringly. "I alone know Fedah, and I alone know how to deal with Sĕra, and how to bring her fat daughter to you in safety. It is I who will go!"

"Send Ebbek to me."

"Not so; I will go myself to Fedah."

"Am I the master, Tadros?"

"You think so, because you are rich. If I knew of the tombs you are plundering, it is I who would be the master!"

"You are in great danger, my poor dragoman."

Tadros, who had been glaring defiantly upon the other, dropped his eyes before the cold look of Kāra.

"Besides, someone must pay old Sĕra the two hundred and fifty piastres due her," he muttered, somewhat confused. "It was the contract, and she will not let the girl come unless she has the money."

"Send Ebbek to me."

The dragoman obeyed. He did not like Kāra's manner. He might, in truth, be in danger if he persisted in protesting. No one was so deep as he in his master's confidence. But what did he know? Merely enough to cause him to fear.

Ebbek performed the mission properly. He not only paid Sĕra her due, but gave her five gold pieces into the bargain, by his master's instructions; and he brought the girl, closely veiled, to Cairo and delivered her to Kāra's housekeeper.

The rooms of the harem had been swept and prepared. They were very luxurious, even for Cairo, and Nephthys was awed by the splendor of the apartments to be devoted to her use. Her dark, serious eyes, glorious as those attributed to the houris of Paradise, wandered about the rooms as she sank upon a divan, too dazed to think or speak.

Neither faculty was a strong point with Nephthys, however. Meekly she had obeyed the summons from the master who had purchased her. She did not try to consider what that summons might mean to her. What use? It was her fate. Perhaps at times she had dimly expected such a change. Kāra had once mentioned to her mother the possibility of his sending for her; but she had not dwelt upon the matter at all.

In the same listless manner that she had carried water from the Nile and worked at the loom she followed old Ebbek to Cairo, leaving her mother to gloat over her store of gold.

The journey across the river was a new experience to her—the journey by railway was wonderful; but she showed no interest. The great eyes calmly saw all, but the brain was not active enough to wonder. She had heard of such things and knew that they existed. Now she saw them—saw marvelous Cairo, with its thousand domes and minarets, its shifting kaleidoscope of street scenes, its brilliant costumes and weird clamor—and the medley of it all dulled her senses.

In a way she was really amused; but the amusement was only sensual. This costume was more gorgeous than the braided jacket of Tadros the dragoman, she observed; that house was better than the one old Hatatcha had lived in. But beyond this vague comparison, the sights were all outside her personal participation in them. The part she herself was playing on the world's great stage, the uncertainty of her immediate future, the reason why this tall, gray-bearded Arab was escorting her to Cairo, were all things she failed to consider.

So it was that on her entry into Kāra's splendid harem the girl could not at first understand that the luxury surrounding her was prepared for her especial use. Had she comprehended this fact, she would still have been unable to imagine why.

She rested upon the cushions and gazed stupidly, yet with childish intentness, at the rich draperies and rugs, the gilded tables and chairs, the marble statuary and the tinkling perfumed fountain in the corner, as if fearing the vision would presently dissolve and she would awake from a dream.

She had brought a bundle under her dark blue shawl, a bundle containing her cotton tunic, the spangled robe and the wreath of artificial flowers. The blue beads Kāra had once given her were around her neck—all but one, which she had carefully removed and given to Sĕra her mother for an amulet.

She scarcely noticed when the old hag who acted as Kāra's housekeeper tossed her precious bundle scornfully into a corner and began to disrobe her. The shawl, the black cotton dress, the coarse undergown, were one by one removed, and then the flat-bottomed home-made shoes.

When she was nude, the hag led her to an adjoining chamber, where her bath was prepared. Nephthys wondered, but did not speak. Neither did old Tilga, the housekeeper. She saw that the girl needed a scrubbing rather than a bath, and gave it to her much as if she were washing a child.

Afterward, when the fat, soft skin was dried, and annointed, and properly perfumed, Tilga led Nephthys to the robing-room, and dressed her in underclothing of silken gauze and a marvelous gown that was fastened with a girdle of cloth of gold. Pink stockings were drawn snugly over her chubby legs, and pink satin slippers, with silver bead-work, adorned her feet.

Then Tilga dressed the girl's magnificent hair, placing a jeweled butterfly against its lustrous coils.

When Nephthys was led before a great mirror, she could scarcely believe the image reflected therein was her own. But the woman in her was at last aroused.

She smiled at herself, then laughed—shyly at first, now with genuine delight. She could have remained hours before the mirror admiring the gorgeous vision; but the hag pulled her away, dragging her by one wrist back to the boudoir, with its gilded furniture and the fountain.

As she sank again upon the divan her eyes saw a tabouret at her side, upon which was a bronze lamp with a floating wick and a tray of cigarettes. She seized one of the latter eagerly, with a half-defiant look at old Tilga, and lighted it from the tiny flame of the lamp. Then she leaned back upon the cushions and inhaled the smoke with perfect enjoyment.

Tilga nodded approval, surveying her new charge the while critically. She had much experience with harems, and wondered where Prince Kāra could have found this exquisite creature; for, to Oriental eyes, at least, Nephthys was rarely beautiful, and, perhaps, few men of Europe would have gazed upon her perfect features and great velvet eyes without admiration.

The rich dress transformed the Nile girl. Her luxurious surroundings but enhanced her beauty. Seemingly she was born for a harem, and fate had qualified her for this experience.

The afternoon that Nephthys arrived, Kāra was at the club, playing écarté with Lord Consinor. He was steadily winning, and in compliance with his usual custom, he declared he would continue to double until he lost.

"I'm not anxious to get your money, Consinor," he remarked, carelessly. "There will doubtless come a change in the luck before long."

The viscount was visibly disturbed. In all his experience he had never seen a man win so persistently. Already the stakes, because of Kāra's system of doubling, were enormous, and the game had attracted a group of spectators, who were almost as eager as the participants.

Gradually the afternoon waned, until at length the prince announced in a low voice that the stakes were ten thousand pounds. Consinor shivered: but with his eyes on the flame-lit ring of the prince, he cut the cards and played his hand as well as he was able. Kāra won, and the viscount threw down the cards with a white face. Already he was ruined, and to risk a deal for twenty thousand pounds was more than his nerves could bear.

"I'm done, Prince," said he, hoarsely.

"Bah! it is nothing," returned Kāra, lightly. "We will merely postpone the play until a more favorable time, when this cursed streak of luck—which I deplore more than you do—is broken. We will start afresh, and you shall have a chance to win your money back. Sign me a note of hand and I will go."

The viscount drew a sheet of paper toward him and signed a note of

L. FRANK BAUM

hand for ten thousand pounds. According to the rules of the club, the paper must be witnessed by two members, so Colonel Varrin and Ering van Roden penciled their initials upon it.

Kāra stuffed the document carelessly into a side pocket; but a moment after, as if struck by a sudden thought, he pulled out a paper and rolled it into a taper. This he lighted from the blaze of a lamp and with it relit his cigar, afterward holding the taper in his fingers until it was consumed to a fine ash. Not a word was spoken. The others watched him silently, but with significant looks, never suspecting he had substituted another paper for the note of hand, while Consinor, as the ash was brushed to the floor, breathed more freely.

"The pleasure of winning ought to be enough for any man," remarked the prince, and, rising from the table, he sauntered from the room.

"Nevertheless, it is a debt of honor," said Colonel Varrin, gravely. "But it is fortunate, Consinor, you were playing with Prince Kāra. The fellow is so confoundedly rich that money means nothing to him, and he will not take his winnings unless you force him to accept them."

"I know that," returned the viscount. "I would never have allowed another man to double the stakes during a winning streak. Perhaps I should not have allowed the prince to do so."

Then he also left the club, for, despite Kāra's seeming generosity in destroying the note, his own insidious nature led him to suspect every man he had dealings with, and the amount involved was so enormous that it would swallow up double the sum his father's crippled estates were now worth. On his own account he had nothing at all beyond the salary he drew from the Ministry of Finance; so he realized his danger, and could not resist feeling that he had been led into a trap.

Meantime Tadros had not forgotten, as his master had done, the probable arrival of Nephthys by the afternoon train. He should have waited in the ante-room of the club for Kāra's orders; but instead he returned to the house and found that the girl had already been there for an hour.

"I will see her," he muttered, and disregarding old Ebbek, who would have stopped him, he entered the harem.

Thrusting aside the draperies, Tadros coolly stalked into the girl's boudoir and then stopped short in undisguised astonishment at what his eyes beheld. Nephthys was reclining upon the divan, smoking her cigarette, resplendent in her fleecy silks, the golden braid and the sparkling jewels.

She smiled and nodded as she saw her old friend the dragoman, but Tilga burst into a flood of angry protestations and curses, rushing at the intruder and trying to drive him from the room with futile pushes of her lean hands.

Tadros resisted, and when the hag started to scream he covered her mouth with his hand, holding her fast at the same time.

"Listen, old imbecile!" he muttered. "Do you wish to lose your place with Prince Kāra? Be sensible, then. You are under my orders—the orders of Tadros the dragoman, and you must obey me."

"I obey only the prince," retorted Tilga, sullenly. "You will not be dragoman when the master hears you have violated his harem."

"Ah, but he will not hear! It is to be our secret, Tilga. You are going to enter my service, and I will make you rich in a few months. See! here are five hundred piastres—five golden pounds in good English money. It is only a promise of more to come. Take it, Tilga."

The hag took it, but with reluctance.

"If the prince discovers—" she began.

"But he won't," declared Tadros, promptly. "He will discover nothing. Just now I left him at the club, playing cards with an Englishman. Go outside, my Tilga, and watch in the courtyard."

She hobbled away, still muttering protests, and the dragoman seated himself upon the divan beside Nephthys.

XIII

THE TALISMAN OF AHTKA-RĀ

Kāra found he had only time to dress for a dinner with Mrs. Everingham. Aneth was to be there also, and he must not neglect the intrigue he was conducting to obtain an ascendency over the girl. That was the reason, he told himself, why he was so anxious to attend.

His plans were progressing well at this time. The only adverse element was the obvious infatuation of Gerald Winston for Miss Consinor; but the Egyptian had carefully gauged the depths of the young girl's character. She was interested in antiquities, and therefore encouraged Winston, who was a noted scholar; but there was no danger in that. Kāra knew more of Egyptology than all the scholars in Cairo, and had often seen Aneth's face brighten when he told her some strange and interesting bit of unwritten history. To be sure, Winston was her own countryman, and had an advantage in that; yet Mrs. Everingham had once said in his hearing that a handsome foreigner was always fascinating to an Englishwoman, and he had remembered the careless remark and pondered its truth until he had come to believe it.

He had a better argument than any of these in reserve, however. If the Englishman really succeeded in winning Aneth's love in the end, then Kāra knew how to compel the girl to obedience.

As he left his room he found the dragoman leaning against a pillar of the courtyard.

"Is Nephthys here?" he inquired.

"I suppose so," answered the dragoman, yawning sleepily. "She was due to arrive this afternoon, wasn't she?"

Kāra looked at him with sudden suspicion.

"Have you seen her?" he demanded.

"Am I the keeper of your harem?" retorted Tadros, indignantly. "Old Tilga has been hidden in the women's quarters for hours. Probably she is attending to your Nephthys."

He eyed his master disdainfully, and Kāra walked on and entered the carriage. He had barely time to join the company at dinner, and Nephthys could wait.

Winston was not present this evening, and the prince found Aneth unusually gracious. She chatted so pleasantly, her manner was so friendly and her clear eyes so sweet and intelligent, that Kāra gave way to the moment's enchantment and forgot all else in the delight of her society.

Nor did he recover readily from the spell. After returning home he paced the floor for an hour, recalling the English girl's fair face and every change of its expression. Then he gave a guilty start as a recollection of Hatatcha swept over him, impressing upon his memory his fearful oath.

Kāra's nature, despite his cold exterior, was fervid in the extreme. He had sworn to hate this girl, yet tonight he loved her passionately. But Hatatcha's training had not entirely failed. He calmed himself, and examined his danger critically, as an outsider might have done.

To yield to his love for Aneth would mean enslavement by the enemy, a condition from which his judgment instinctively revolted. To steel his heart against her charms would be difficult, but its necessity was obvious. He determined to pursue his plot with relentless hatred, and to raise between the girl and himself as many bars as possible. He scorned his own weakness, and since he knew that it existed, he resolved to conquer it.

Once Hatatcha had said to him: "You are cold, selfish and cruel, and I have made you so." True; these qualities had been carefully instilled into his nature. He was proud that he possessed them, for he had a mission to fulfil. And if he desired any peace in his future life, that mission must be fully accomplished.

In the morning he went to see Nephthys, and his face brightened as he realized how remarkably beautiful she was. The Orientals generally admire only the form of a woman, being indifferent to the face; but Kāra was modern enough to appreciate beauty of feature, while holding to an extent the Eastern prejudice that a fat and soft form is the chief attraction of the female sex. So he found Nephthys admirable in every way; and if her indifference and perfect subjection to his will in anyway annoyed him, he was at this time unaware of the fact. He wished this girl to replace Aneth Consinor in his affection and esteem, and would forgive much in Nephthys if she could manage to bring about this excellent result.

After this he devoted much of his attention to the Nile girl, striving in his association with her to exclude all outside interests. He purchased for her marvelous costumes and hired two Arab maidens to attend her

L. FRANK BAUM

and keep her royally attired. Kāra's most splendid diamonds and rubies were set by Andalaft in many coronets, brooches and bracelets to deck her person, and many of the wonderful pearls he had brought from the secret tomb were carefully sized and strung to form a necklace for the Egyptian girl's portly neck.

Nephthys was pleased with these possessions. They drew her from the dull lassitude in which she had existed, and aroused in her breast a womanly exultation that even her mother could never have imagined her able to develop. It may be the girl began to think and to dream; yet if so, there was little outward indication of the fact. To comprehend any woman's capabilities is difficult; to comprehend those of Nephthys seemed impossible. She was luxury-loving by nature, as are all Orientals, and accepted the comforts of her surroundings without questioning why they were bestowed upon her. Whatever sensibilities she possessed had long lain dormant. They might be awakening now; her delight in adornment seemed the first step in that direction.

Kāra purposely remained away from the club for several evenings following that in which he had won Consinor's ten thousand pounds. Perhaps he wished his enemy to become uneasy and fret at the delay in wiping out the debt, and if so, it would have gratified him to know the feverish anxiety with which the viscount haunted the club, and watched every new arrival in the hope that Kāra would appear.

At last the Egyptian judged that he had waited long enough, and prepared to still further enmesh his victim. In his room that evening he took from a secret drawer of his cabinet a small roll of papyrus, on which were closely written hieroglyphics. To refresh his memory he read the scroll carefully, although it was not the first time he had studied it since it had fallen at his feet when the bust of Isis was overturned at the tomb of Ahtka-Rā.

Freely translated, the writing was as follows:

"Being finally prepared to join Anubis in the nether world, I, Ahtka-Rā, son of the Sun and High Priest of Āmen, have caused to be added to the decoration of my sarcophagus the precious Stone of Fortune given to me by the King of Kesh[1] in return for having preserved him and his people from the wrath of Rameses. It is my belief that this wondrous stone will guard my tomb when my spirit has departed, and by its powers preserve my body and my treasure from being despoiled,

---

1. Ethiopia.

until that time when I shall return to Qemt[2] to live again. Let no descendant of my house remove it from its place, for the Stone of Fortune is mine, and I bequeath it not to any of those who may come after me. In time of need my children may take of the treasure what they require, but to disturb my Stone of Fortune will be to draw upon the offender the bitterest curse of my spirit. It may be known to all from its changing color, being never the same for long; and the color of it is not bright, as is the ruby or the carnelian or amethyst, but ever gloomy and mysterious. That none may mistake its location, I have embedded it in a triple band of gold, and it is placed at the head of my sarcophagus. There shall it remain. Since it came into my possession I have ever worn it in my bosom, and by its magic I have been able to control Rameses the son of Seti, to rule his kingdom as if it were my own, to confound all my enemies and accusers, and to amass such riches as no man of Qemt has ever before possessed. Also has it brought to me health and many years in which to accomplish the purpose of my present existence. For this reason do I refuse to part with it in the ages during which I await the new life. Whatever else may happen to my tomb, I implore those who live in the days to come to leave to me this one treasure."

It was signed by Ahtka-Rā and sealed with his seal, being doubtless the work of his own hand.

Kāra rerolled the papyrus and put it away, pausing to glance with a smile at the strange ring he wore upon his hand.

"My great ancestor was selfish," he murmured, "and wished to prevent any of his descendants from becoming as famous as he himself was. Nevertheless, had I read the script before I removed the stone from the sarcophagus, I would have respected Ahtka-Rā's wish; but I did not know what treasure I had gained until afterward, when it was too late to restore the stone without another visit to the tomb. A curse is a dreadful thing, especially from one's ancestor, and it is even to avoid Hatatcha's curse that I am now fulfilling her vengeance. But Ahtka-Rā may rest content; I have merely borrowed his talisman, and it shall be returned to him when I have obtained full satisfaction from my grandmother's enemies. Meantime, the stone will protect me from evil fortune, and when it is restored the curse will be averted."

Something in this expression struck him as incongruous. He thought deeply for a moment, a frown gathering upon his brow. Then he said:

2. Egypt.

L. FRANK BAUM

"I must not deceive myself with sophistries. What if the curse is already working, and because of it the English girl has turned my strength to weakness? But that cannot be. Whenever I have worn this ring I have mastered all difficulties and triumphed as I desired; and I will triumph in my undertaking tonight, in spite of the reproach I can already see in Aneth's eyes. I am still the controller of my own destiny as well as the destinies of others; for if the talisman did so much for Ahtka-Rā as he claims, it will surely prove stronger than any curse."

With a laugh he shook off the uncanny feeling that had for the moment oppressed him, and went to the club.

XIV

Rogues Ancient and Modern

Consinor arrived early at the Lotus Club and took his seat at a small table facing the doorway, where he whiled away the time by playing solitaire.

Presently Kāra entered and greeted him cordially, seeming to be in an especially happy mood.

"Well, shall we try our luck?" he said, seating himself at the opposite side of the table.

Nodding assent, Consinor gathered up the cards and shuffled them. Several loungers who knew of the previous game and wondered what the next meeting between the two men would evolve, clustered around the table to watch the result.

Kāra won the cut and dealt. He played rather carelessly and lost. The stakes were a pound sterling.

"Double!" he cried, laughing, and again the viscount nodded.

The luck had shifted, it seemed, for the prince repeatedly lost. At first he chatted gaily with those present and continued to double with reckless disregard of his opponent's success; but by and by he grew thoughtful and looked at his cards more closely, watching the game as shrewdly as his adversary. The stakes had grown to four hundred pounds, and a subtle thrill of excitement spread over the little group of watchers. Was Consinor going to win back his ten thousand pounds at one sitting?

Suddenly Kāra, in dealing, fumbled the cards and dropped one of them. In reaching to pick it up it slipped beneath his foot and he tore it into two. It was the queen of hearts.

"How stupid!" he laughed, showing the pieces. "Here, boy, bring us a fresh pack of cards," addressing an attendant.

Consinor scowled and reached out his hand for the now useless deck. Kāra slipped the cards into his pocket, including the mutilated one.

"They are mine, prince," said the viscount; "I use them for playing my game of solitaire."

"Pardon, but I have destroyed their value," returned Kāra. "I shall insist upon presenting you with a new deck, since my awkwardness has rendered your own useless."

Consinor bit his lip, but made no reply, watching silently while the prince tore open the new deck and shuffled the cards.

The viscount lost the next hand, and the score was evened. He lost again, and still a third time.

"The luck has changed with the new cards," said he. "Let us postpone the game until another evening, unless you prefer to continue."

"Very well," Kāra readily returned, and throwing down the cards, he leaned back in his chair, selected a fresh cigar from his case and carefully lighted it.

Consinor had pushed back his own chair, but he did not rise. After watching Kāra's nonchalant movements for a time, the viscount drew from his pocket three curious dice, and after an instant's hesitation tossed them upon the table.

"Here is a curiosity," he remarked. "I am told these cubes were found in an Egyptian tomb at Thebes. They are said to be three thousand years old."

The men present, including Kāra, examined the dice curiously. The spots were arranged much as they are at the present day, an evidence that this mode of gambling has been subjected to little improvement since the early Egyptians first invented it.

"They are excellently preserved," said van Roden. "Where did you get them, viscount?"

"I picked them up the other day from a strolling Arab. They seemed to me very quaint."

"There are several sets in the museum," remarked Pintsch, a German in charge of the excavations at Dashur. "It is very wonderful how much those ancients knew."

Lord Consinor drew the dice toward him.

"See here, Prince," said he, "let us try our luck with these antiquities. It is quicker and easier than écarté."

"Very well," consented Kāra. "What are the stakes?"

"Let us say a hundred pounds the throw."

This suggestion startled the group of spectators; but Kāra said at once:

"I will agree to that, my lord."

He lost once, twice, thrice.

Then, as Consinor, with a triumphant leer, pushed the dice toward him, Kāra thrust his hands in his pockets and said in a quiet voice to the onlookers:

"Gentlemen, I call upon you to witness that I am playing with a rogue. These dice are loaded."

Following a moment's horrified silence, the viscount sprang up with an oath.

"This is an insult, Prince Kāra!" he cried.

"Sit down," said Colonel Varrin, sternly. "No mere words can condemn you, sir. Let us examine the dice."

The others concurred, their faces bearing witness to their dismay and alarm. Such a disgraceful occurrence had never before been known within those eminently respectable walls. The honor of the club was, they felt, at stake.

The cubes were carefully tested. It was as Kāra had charged—they were loaded.

"Can you explain this, Lord Consinor?" asked one of the party.

"I cannot see why I should be called upon to explain," was the reply. "In purchasing the dice, I was wholly ignorant of their condition. It was a mere impulse that led me to offer to play with them."

"It is well known that these ancient dice are frequently loaded," interrupted Pintsch, eagerly, as if he saw a solution of the affair. "Two of the sets exhibited in the museum have been treated in the same clever manner."

"That is true," agreed Varrin, nodding gravely.

"In that case," said Consinor, "I am sure you gentlemen will exonerate me from any intentional wrong. It is simply my misfortune that I offered to play with the dice."

"Was it also your misfortune, my lord," returned Kāra, calmly, "that you have been playing all the evening with marked cards? I will ask you to explain to these gentlemen why this deck, which you have claimed in their presence to be your private property, bears secret marks that could only have been placed there with one intent—to swindle an unsuspecting antagonist."

He drew the cards from his pocket as he spoke and handed them to Colonel Varrin, who examined them with a troubled countenance and then turned them over to his neighbor for inspection.

While the cards passed around, Consinor sat staring blankly at the group. The evidence against him was so incontrovertible that he saw no means of escape from the disgrace which was sure to follow.

"Gentlemen," said Kāra, when the last man had examined the cards and laid them upon the table again, "I trust you will all bear evidence that it is not my usual custom or desire to win money from those I play with. Rather do I prefer to lose, for in that way I obtain the

amusement of playing, without the knowledge that I may have inconvenienced my friends. But when a common trickster and cheat conspires to rob me, my temper is different. Lord Consinor owes me ten thousand pounds, and I demand from him in your presence prompt payment of the debt. Also, I depend upon you to protect me and my fellow-members from card sharpers in the future, which I am sure you will gladly do. For the rest, the matter is in your hands. Good evening, gentlemen."

He bowed with dignity and withdrew. The others silently followed, scattering to other rooms of the club. Varrin, as a club official, took with him the incriminating dice and the marked cards.

Lord Consinor, knowing well that he was ruined, sat muttering curses upon Kāra and his own "hard luck" until he noticed the deserted room and decided to go home. The disaster had fairly dazed him, so that he failed to realize the fact that as he called for his hat and coat in the lobby the groups of bystanders ceased their eager talk and carefully turned their backs in his direction.

The viscount had never heard of Hatatcha; yet it was her vengeance that had overtaken him.

XV

Winston Bey is Indignant

In their rooms at the Savoy next morning Lord Roane and his son quarreled violently. The day's paper contained a full account of the affair at the club, and while no names were mentioned, there was no misunderstanding who the culprit was. "An English nobleman who had lately arrived to fill an important position in the Ministry of Finance was detected playing with marked cards and loaded dice by a well-known Egyptian gentleman of wealth and high station, who promptly exposed the fraud in the presence of several reputable club members. Fortunately, the Englishman's name had only been posted and he had not yet been admitted to membership in the club, so that his trickery and consequent disgrace in no way reflects upon that popular and admirably conducted institution, etc."

Lord Roane was vastly chagrined and indignant as he read the account.

"You low, miserable scoundrel!" he roared, facing his son; "how dare you drag the name of your family in the mire, just as we are assuming an indisputable position of respectability in Cairo? To be a gambler is despicable enough, but to become a common cheat and swindler is utterly unpardonable. What have you to say for yourself?"

"Nothing," said Consinor, sullenly. "I am innocent. It was a plot to ruin me."

"Pah! a plot of yours to ruin others rather. Speak up, man! Have you nothing to say to excuse or palliate your shame and dishonor?"

"What use?" asked the viscount, apathetically. "You will not believe me."

"Do you believe him, Aneth?" asked the old man, turning to gaze upon the girl's horrified face. "Do you believe that this cur, who is my son and your father, is innocent?"

"No," she answered, shrinking back as Consinor looked up curiously to hear her reply. "He has deceived me cruelly. He promised me he would not touch a card again, or play for money, and he has broken his word. I cannot believe him now."

"Of course not," her father retorted, reddening for the first time. "My precious family is so rotten throughout that even its youngest member cannot give a Consinor credit for being honest or sincere."

"See here, Roger; I will not have Aneth insulted, even by you. I'm not a saint, I'll admit; but I've never been guilty of petty swindling, and your daughter is pure enough to shame us both. As for you, I've done with you, and you must from this time work out your salvation in your own way. You've dissipated any inheritance you might have had; but I'll give you a thousand pounds in cash if you'll take your ugly face out of Cairo and promise not to come near us again. I'll take care of your wife and daughter, neither of whom, I am positive, will miss you for a single hour."

"It's a good offer," said Consinor, quickly, "and I'll accept it. Where did you get the thousand pounds?"

"That," declared my lord, stiffly, "is none of your accursed business! Now go. Leave your resignation with the Minister of Finance and then make yourself scarce. Here, I'll write you a check now."

Consinor took the paper.

"If it is good, and the bank will cash it," he said, slowly, "I'll do as I have agreed, and not trouble you again. Goodbye, Aneth. Look out for that snakey Egyptian who is following you around. He alone is responsible for this affair, and you cannot afford to trust him; and give my fond farewell to your mother. She won't mind if I do not appear in person to irritate her nerves."

"Where will you go?" asked Lord Roane.

"That, sir, to repeat your own words, is none of your accursed business."

With this filial response he left the room, and Aneth burst into a flood of tears. Never had she felt so wretched and humiliated as at this discovery of her father's infamy, and although Roane tried to comfort his granddaughter by pointing out the fact that Roger had long been a gambler with a character not above suspicion, the girl had so fondly hoped for her father's regeneration that her disappointment was indeed bitter.

"It won't hurt us so very much, my child," continued the old nobleman, stroking her head soothingly. "The world will know we have repudiated Roger, and will sympathise with our distress. In a few months the scandal will be forgotten, and we may again hold up our heads. I'm afraid I've lived a rather wicked life, my dear; but for your sake I would like to retrieve my good name and die possessed of the honor and respect of all my fellow-men. And this, I believe, I can accomplish. Don't worry, little one! Be brave, and the blow will not hurt half so much."

There were tears in his own eyes as he marked her distress, and he continued to encourage her until the young girl had partly recovered her self-control and the first shock of her sudden misfortune had been blunted. Then he kissed her tenderly and went away to his office.

The account in the morning paper had likewise caused Gerald Winston considerable amazement and dismay. His first thought was of Aneth and the trouble that had come to her; his next a feeling of resentment toward Kāra. After pacing the floor restlessly for an hour, he called for his saddle-horse and rode down the Shubra road to interview the Egyptian at his villa.

Kāra was at home and received his visitor with cold politeness, which Winston passed unnoticed. He was not in a mood to be affected by trifles.

"I understand that you accused Consinor of cheating at the club last night," he began, impetuously.

"Well?" said Kāra, lifting his brows inquiringly.

"Why did you do it?"

"Because it was true. He was robbing me."

"You know what I mean, sir! You have been posing as a friend of Miss Consinor. To expose her father to public shame was the act of a cowardly enemy."

"What would you have done in my place?" asked Kāra, calmly.

"I? I would have concealed the discovery and allowed the man to go, refusing to play with him again," declared Winston.

"And so have allowed him to rob others, perhaps?"

"If necessary, yes, that his daughter's good name might be protected. But a private warning would have induced him to abandon further trickery."

"He is an old offender, I believe," said Kāra, leaning back in his chair and regarding the other with an amused expression. "It might benefit you to reflect that Miss Consinor's good name has not been acquired on account of her father's respectability, anymore than through the reputation of her grandsire, who has grown old in iniquity. Therefore, I cannot believe that I have injured her in anyway."

A tinge of passionate hatred in the man's voice as he referred to Lord Roane aroused Winston's attention. Then, suddenly, a light broke upon him.

L. FRANK BAUM

"See here, Kāra," he said, sternly, "are you persecuting these people and plotting against them because of the old wrong that Roane did your grandmother, Hatatcha?"

"I am neither persecuting nor plotting against them," declared Kāra. "Consinor has ruined himself unaided. As for his daughter, I have every object in protecting her from scandal."

"What do you mean by that, sir?"

"I intend to marry her."

At this cool statement Winston stared aghast. Then he gave a bitter laugh.

"That is absurd and impossible," he said.

"Why so?"

"You are cousins."

"She does not know that, and you will not tell her because you have so much regard for her grandfather's good name," with a sneer.

"I see. It is your plot to ruin her; but it will fail, because she will never consent to marry you," he continued.

"How do you know that?" asked Kāra.

"It is improbable that she can love you."

"In that, sir, I am inclined to differ with you. Even if Aneth discovered our relationship, it would not matter. In olden days our Egyptian kings married their sisters. And I suppose that Lord Roane would emphatically deny the assertion that I am his grandson. I would myself deny it, and you have no proof to back your statement of the fact."

"You told me the story with your own lips."

"To be sure—and the story was true. I do not mind acknowledging it at this moment, because there are no witnesses present; but if you repeat the statement in public, I will deny it absolutely."

For a moment Winston remained thoughtfully silent. Then he said:

"You are proposing a dreadful crime, Kāra, but it will avail you nothing to defy morality in this way. There is another reason why Miss Consinor will refuse to marry you, and it is entirely distinct from the subject of your relationship."

"To what do you refer?"

"To the woman you are keeping, even now, in your harem. It is a matter of public scandal, and I am surprised that society has not already ostracized you for your audacious defiance of propriety. You are neither an Arab nor a Mohammedan. Doubtless the offense has not yet come to Miss Consinor's ears; but if it does, have you any idea she would place her happiness in the hands of a man of your character?"

Kāra frowned. Here was a weapon against him that he had never before recognized.

"I suppose you will take pains to inform Miss Consinor that I have a slave-girl among my servants," he said, mockingly.

"I shall ask Mrs. Everingham to tell her the truth concerning your domestic relations," returned Winston, decidedly.

The Egyptian arose.

"I think it will be as well to end this interview, Winston Bey," he said. "You are yourself a pretender for the hand of my future bride, and it is useless to endeavor to fairly discuss matters wherein you are so selfishly concerned."

"Do you choose to defy my warnings?" asked Winston, angrily.

"By no means. I merely ignore your implied threats. They can in no way interfere with my plans."

"I believe," said Winston, striving to control his indignation, "that those plans are inspired by hatred rather than love. I shall do my best to oppose them."

"Naturally. It is your privilege, sir."

Winston turned to go.

"I shall always regret," he remarked, bitterly, as a parting shot, "that I was so foolish as to bring a filthy native from out the natural environment of his mud village."

"The filthy native would have found other means of escape had you not brought him; so you need not reproach yourself," returned Kāra, with a smile. "But the trifle you have mentioned should not be your deepest regret, my stupid Englishman!"

"Did I do anything more foolish?"

"Yes."

"What was it?"

"You kicked me twice beneath the palms of Fedah."

"Ah! I should not have restrained myself to two kicks."

"Be content, sir. Twice was sufficient, since it is liable to cause you much unhappiness. I had it in mind, had you kicked me again, to kill you."

Winston left the villa more thoughtful than he had been on his arrival. The matter involved much more, it seemed, than the loss of Lord Consinor's reputation. Kāra's confident tone had not failed to impress his rival, and the Englishman was more uneasy than he cared to admit even to himself. His love for Aneth was sincere and unselfish, and he could imagine no greater calamity for the girl than to acquire a fondness for the treacherous native whose presence he had just left. Such a contingency had not occurred to him before, and for this reason Kāra's claims were as startling as they were revolting. He longed to go to the girl at once and strive to comfort her in this, her hour of sorrow; but a natural delicacy restrained him. She would like to be alone, at first, until she had somewhat recovered from the humiliation she would be sure to suffer at the public exposure of her father's misdeeds. Afterward he could assure her of his confidence and friendship, and, when the proper time came, of his love. Meantime he contented himself by sending Aneth a basket of the most beautiful roses to be found in Cairo.

No such delicacy of feeling influenced Kāra. In the afternoon he went to the Savoy and sent up his card.

Aneth was alone, Mrs. Everingham having just left her for a drive. The girl received the Egyptian almost with eagerness.

"Can you forgive me, Prince?" she asked, by way of greeting, as she stood before him with scarlet cheeks and downcast eyes.

"Forgive you for what, Miss Aneth?" he replied, gently.

"For—for the wrong my father did you," she stammered.

Kāra smiled, and she glanced up shyly in time to catch his expression of amusement.

"Let us sit down and talk it over," he said, taking her hand and leading her to a chair. "But it will be unnecessary, I am sure, for me to say that I have nothing to forgive, since you have in no way offended."

"But my father—" she began, timidly, again dropping her eyes in shame.

"Yes, I know, Miss Aneth," said he. "Your father did a foolish thing, for which people will justly condemn him. I am very sorry that it was through me he was detected, but I assure you I was powerless to prevent it. Others saw the marked cards and forced the accusation against him. Believe me, I would have saved him if possible; but I could not."

"I believe you, Prince Kāra," she said. "It was all my father's fault, and his punishment is only such as he deserved."

"I am deeply grieved for your sake," continued Kāra, and indeed the sight of her sweet face, convulsed with anguish, so appealed to him at the moment that his speech was almost sincere. "I know what this disgrace will mean to you, Aneth—the avoidance of your former associates, and the jeers, perhaps, of those who have envied you. The world is heartless always, and visits the sins of the fathers upon their children; so that your innocence will not be considered save by your truest friends."

He paused, for she was crying now, softly but miserably, and the tears moved him strangely.

"That is why I have come," he continued, his voice trembling with earnestness, "to assure you of my faith in you and of my steadfast friendship. Nay, more; I offer to protect you against the sneers of all the world, if you will grant me the right."

The girl started, glancing nervously and almost affrightedly into his face.

"I—I do not understand you, Prince Kāra," she murmured.

"Then I must speak more plainly," he quickly rejoined, springing up to stand before her with sparkling eyes and outstretched hands.

"Aneth, my sweet one, I love you! To me you represent the joys of earth and the delights of paradise. Only in your presence do I find happiness and content. Be my wife, Aneth; give me yourself, and I will guard you so well and place you so high that all the world will bow at your feet."

The speech shocked her, for there was no mistaking the man's earnestness. Nor did she know how to reply, the proposal being as unexpected as it was inopportune. Aneth may have had vague dreams of love, as maidens will and should have; but she had been so happy in Cairo that she had not thought the attentions of Kāra meant more than the kindly good-fellowship of the other men she had met. Indeed, she had not considered such a subject at all, and at this hour, when her heart was wrung with grief, she found in it no response to her suitor's fervid appeals.

"I cannot reply to you just now, Prince Kāra," she said, with hesitation; "it is all new to me, and quite unexpected, and—and I do not wish to marry anyone."

His face hardened as he gazed upon her timid, shrinking form, but the longing in his dark eyes remained. With all his lately acquired polish, the native failed to comprehend that an English girl does not yield herself to the demands of any man unless her heart and inclinations lead her to acknowledge his authority. But he was wise enough to perceive that the difficulties of the situation required tact if he wished to succeed.

"Aneth," said he, more quietly, "this is no time for evasions or misunderstandings between us. I have told you that I love you, that my earnest desire is to make you my wife. You need a protector at this moment, and a delay is as foolish as it is dangerous to your interests. If you love me at all, you can tell me so today as well as later."

"Ah, that is it, Prince! I'm afraid that I do not love you in the way that you wish," answered the girl, aroused to a more dignified tone by his persistence. "I am very grateful to you, Prince Kāra, and appreciate the honor of your proposal; but I have nothing more to offer you than my sincere friendship."

"Then I will accept that as sufficient for the time being," said he. "I will marry your friendship, Aneth, and perhaps the love will sometime follow."

"Oh, I cannot allow that!" she cried, distressed. "I am sorry to hurt you when you are so kind to me; but can't you see that I am unnerved and unhappy today, and that if you force me to answer you, I can only say 'no'?"

He grew thoughtful at this, studying her features carefully. After a moment he replied:

"I will not press the question further now, but will give you two days for consideration. Will you answer me at the end of that time?"

She hesitated, knowing already what the answer would be and that it was best he understood her at once. Yet to her inexperienced mind it seemed more easy to postpone the matter until she had time to collect her thoughts and reply to Kāra more gently and effectively.

"Yes," said she, answering him; "come to me in two days, please."

To her surprise he bowed gravely and at once left the room; but the relief she experienced made her glad that she had found this simple way to evade her present difficulties. In two days she would know better what to say to him.

Kāra was astonished at his own forbearance. Where he might have threatened and compelled he had merely implored, and he could not in the least understand the mood that had swayed his actions. But while in the girl's presence he seemed not to be himself, or even to know himself.

If only Aneth would love him, how gladly would he shield her from the inheritance of his grandmother's malignant vengeance! Even if she could not love him, he was determined to win her for his wife, for the longing of his heart was at this time too great to be denied.

In her tears and distress the girl had seemed more lovely than ever, and, as he drove slowly homeward, he dwelt upon her with an ecstasy of adoration that seemed entirely foreign to his cold and calculating nature. At this moment perhaps he really loved Aneth; but the Eastern lover is prone to sudden fits of intense passion that soon exhaust themselves, and the reaction is apt to restore them to their native apathy with surprising abruptness.

When Kāra arrived home he at once crossed the courtyard and entered the quarters devoted to women. Ever since Winston had sneered at his relations with Nephthys that morning, the thing had rankled in his mind, and now, fresh from Aneth's presence, he reproached himself for his folly in bringing the stupid Nile girl to Cairo. For, in spite of his efforts to amuse himself in her society, Nephthys had not only proved unable to destroy his love for Aneth, but her quiescent indifference, beautiful though she was, served rather to disgust him by its sharp contrast with the English girl's brightness and innocence.

Never doubting that he would shortly install Aneth in Nephthys' place, he suddenly resolved to have done with the Egyptian girl, who had been so great a disappointment to him.

There was a dark scowl upon Kāra's face as he pushed aside the draperies and entered the apartment of Nephthys. He found the girl seated upon her divan, with the dragoman comfortably established beside her. Both were smoking cigarettes and Tadros was holding Nephthys with one arm loosely clasped around her waist.

They did not notice the master's presence for a moment; but when they looked up, Kāra was standing before them with folded arms. The frown had vanished, and his expression was one of positive content; for here was his excuse.

"Tadros," said he, in a soft voice, "be good enough to go into the courtyard. You may wait there for me."

The dragoman stood up and flicked the ash from his cigarette. He was evidently much disturbed.

"If you think, Kāra—" he began, in a very loud, boisterous voice.

"Go into the courtyard, please," interrupted the other, quietly.

Tadros hesitated and glanced at Nephthys. The girl was staring with frightened eyes into her master's face. Following her gaze, the dragoman gave a shudder. Kāra's countenance was as cold and inexpressive as that of a statue. Tadros had learned to fear that expression. Softly he tiptoed from the room, and the draperies fell behind him.

Clinging to the curtains of the arch leading to the next room, appeared old Tilga, who was trembling violently. Had the master been an Arab, her life was already forfeited. She was not sure what an Egyptian would do under the circumstances.

Kāra beckoned her to approach. Then, pointing a finger at Nephthys, he said:

"Remove those jewels and ornaments."

As the old woman eagerly attempted to obey, Nephthys stood up and asked in a low, horrified voice:

"What are you going to do?"

Kāra did not reply. He watched Tilga's nervous fingers rapidly removing the diadem, earrings, brooches and bracelets, which she cast in a heap upon a table. Nephthys submitted quietly until the hag seized her string of pearls; then she shrank away and clutched at her throat to save her treasure, loving the pearls better than all else.

Kāra grasped her wrists firmly and drew her hands down to her side, while Tilga unwound the triple row of priceless pearls from the girl's neck and added it to the heap upon the table. He continued to hold her fast until the housekeeper had stripped from her fingers the rings of diamond, ruby and emerald. Then he let her go, and Nephthys moaned and covered her face with her hands.

"Take off her robes," commanded Kāra, sternly.

Tilga rushed to do his bidding, and, when Nephthys resisted, the hag struck her across the face with her open hand. She literally tore away the exquisite gown, as well as the silken hose and satin slippers, until the girl stood shorn of all her finery except the fleecy underclothing.

"Leave her that," said Kāra. "And now, where is her black cotton dress?"

Tilga hurriedly fetched it from a closet in the robing chamber. She brought the head-shawl and the coarse shoes also.

Nephthys was sobbing now as miserably as a child that has been robbed of its toys.

"I won't wear them! I won't have them! Take them away!" she wailed, as the old Fedah garments were produced.

But the woman shook her angrily and slapped her again, covering her with the crude, soiled gown, and then pushing her back upon the divan while she placed the flat shoes upon the girl's bare feet. Tears were still standing in Nephthys' great eyes, but she submitted to the inevitable with a resumption of her old obedient manner.

"Call Ebbek," said the master; and Tilga displayed such activity that she quickly returned, dragging the Arab after her.

"You will take this woman back to Fedah, whence you brought her, and deliver her over to her mother again. There is a train at sundown, and you will be able to catch it if you are prompt. Drive to the station in a carriage."

Ebbek bowed without betraying surprise at his master's unexpected command. Perhaps he had been observant, and knew the reason for the girl's dismissal.

"Must old Sĕra return your money?" he asked.

"No; tell her she may keep it. Here is gold for your expenses. Feed Nephthys at the railway station, if you have time, and buy her some cigarettes. Now hasten."

Ebbek took the girl's arm to lead her away. As she passed Kāra she halted to say, with despairing intensity:

"I hate you! Some day I will kill you."

Kāra laughed. He was in a pleased mood.

"Goodbye, Nephthys," he rejoined, complacently. "Tell Sĕra I present you to her with my compliments."

Then he left the room and found Tadros standing stiffly outside the door.

"Follow me," he said, and the dragoman obeyed.

He led the way to his own room and sat down facing the dragoman.

Tadros remained standing. He held in his hand the stump of a half-burned cigarette, which he eyed critically and with an air of absorbing interest.

Kāra, being amused, remained silent.

After a time the dragoman coughed to clear his throat.

"You see, Kāra," he began, "I bought the girl first, and paid good money for her when I was desperately poor—a fact that deserves some consideration; yet you forced me to sell her."

"Indeed!"

"Yes, for an insignificant roll of papyrus. I don't complain, having accepted the bargain; but you mustn't blame me for all that has happened. By the beard of Osiris! is a man's heart to be bought and sold like a woman's body? It is absurd."

He paused, shifting from one foot to the other. Then he lifted his eyes, and was pained to find Kāra staring at him fixedly.

"There should be no quarrel between us," he continued, striving to speak confidently. "I have been your jackal, and did your dirty work for a fair amount of pay. What then? To ruin me will cause your own

L. FRANK BAUM

downfall. You dare not do it. But I am honest with you, and a good servant. You need not fear me in the future, for I will promise you on my word to avoid your harem—the word of Tadros the dragoman!"

As he spoke, a shrill scream reached their ears. Tadros bounded to the window, and through the lattice saw Ebbek pushing the unhappy Nephthys into a carriage. He turned a frowning face toward his master.

"What are you doing to the girl?" he demanded, fiercely.

"Sending her back to Sĕra."

The dragoman uttered a curse and made for the door.

"Come here!" cried Kāra, sternly.

Tadros stopped, hesitated, and then returned. He realized that he could do nothing.

"Very well," said he, sullenly. "She will be safer in Fedah than in Cairo. But you have been cruel, Kāra. A man who is really a man would not treat a beast as you have treated Nephthys. To teach her the splendid luxury of a palace and then thrust her back into a mud hut on the forsaken Nile bank is a positive crime! I suppose you have also taken away her fine clothes and her pretty ornaments?"

"Yes."

"Poor child! But there—one does not argue with a snake for fear of its venom. I am likewise in your power," said the dragoman, gloomily.

Kāra actually laughed at his rueful expression.

"You were born a fool, my Tadros," said he, "and a fool you will die. Look you! there is no excuse in all your chatter to me of your own treachery—the crime that our customs declare merits death. You simply accuse me of harshness in sending away a faithless woman. Tell me, then, some plausible reason why I should not kill you."

Tadros grew pale.

"There are two reasons," he replied, seriously. "One is that murdering me would cause you to get into trouble with the police. The other is that you have need of me."

"Very good. The first argument does not count, because you could be killed secretly, with no personal danger to me; and that, without doubt, is the manner in which I shall kill you some day. But your present safety, my Tadros, lies in your second reason. I still need your services, and will permit you to remain alive until I am quite sure to have no further use for you."

The dragoman drew a long breath.

"Let us forget it, Kāra," said he. "I admit that I have been somewhat indiscreet; but what then? All men are indiscreet at times, and you will cease to blame me when you discover how faithful I am to your interests."

Kāra did not reply. The carriage had long since driven away. The dragoman again shifted his position uneasily.

"May I go?" he asked.

"Yes."

And Tadros withdrew, his heart filled with fear and hatred; but the hatred remained long after the fear had subsided.

XVI

KĀRA THREATENS

Those two days were uneasy ones to Kāra. He felt no dread of Aneth's final answer, but the waiting for it was wearisome. Their arrangements might easily have been concluded at the last interview had he not been weak enough to defer to the girl's foolish desire to postpone the inevitable. Since he had come from Fedah, the world had been his plaything, and he found it in no way difficult to accomplish those things he determined upon. He had, therefore, acquired unbounded confidence in the powers of Ahtka-Rā's remarkable Stone of Fortune, which he believed to have a strong influence over all his undertakings. So the Egyptian merely sought to occupy his time to good advantage until he could bring his bride—willing or unwilling mattered little—home to his handsome villa.

He sent Tadros to summon the most famous merchants of Cairo to wait upon him, and arranged to have the women's quarters redecorated in regal fashion. He selected many rich silks and embroideries for Aneth's use when she should need them, and secured an increased corps of Arab servants, well trained in their duties, to attend the slightest wish of their new mistress. He realized that the establishment must hereafter be conducted more upon the plan of a modern European household, and that the apartments of the harem must be transformed into parlors, reception-halls and drawing-rooms.

In marrying Aneth he determined to abandon all Oriental customs and adopt the manners of the newer and broader civilization. He would exhibit his wife in society, and, through her, gain added distinction. His villa would become renowned for its fêtes and magnificent hospitality. Such a life appealed to his imagination, and a marriage with the English girl rendered it possible.

Hatatcha had educated and trained Kāra for a purpose; but now her mission and his oath to fulfil it were alike disregarded. He had given the matter considerable thought recently, and decided that his love for Aneth Consinor canceled all obligations to persecute her or her people further. Hatatcha was dead and forgotten by the world, and her wrongs could never be righted by any vengeance that he might inflict upon her enemies. She could not appreciate the justice of retribution, since her spirit was far away in the nether world with Anubis, and her body in the tombs of Fedah. He had, at first, been conscientious in his determination to accomplish his grandmother's will, but a girl's eyes had thwarted him, and Hatatcha had herself proved weak when love assailed her. Even as all his schemes were approaching fruition and his grandmother's revenge was nearing accomplishment, the compelling power of his love arrested his hand and induced him to cast aside everything that might interfere with his prospective happiness.

On the afternoon of the second day he dressed himself carefully and ordered his chauffeur to be ready to drive him to the Savoy; but as he was about to leave his room, a note was brought to him from Aneth. He tore it open and eagerly read the message—

> Dear Prince Kāra
>
> I am not going to risk another unpleasant interview, because I am anxious we should remain in the future, as in the past, good friends and comrades. But please do not again ask me to marry you, for such a thing is utterly impossible. While I am glad to enjoy your friendship, I can never return the love you profess to bear me, and without love a true woman will not marry. So I beg you will forget that such a thing has ever been discussed between us, and forbear to refer to it again.
>
> Your friend,
> ANETH CONSINOR

As he read the note Kāra's face grew set and stern and his dark eyes flashed ominously. He read it a second time, with more care, trying to find some word of hope or compromise in the frankly written epistle. But there was none.

He experienced a sensation of disappointment and chagrin, tinged with considerable astonishment. Strange as it may seem, he had never for a moment anticipated such a positive refusal. But his nature was impetuous and capricious, and presently anger drove all other feelings from his heart; and the anger grew and expanded until it was hot and furious and took full possession of him.

Perhaps it was the blow to his self-esteem that was most effective in destroying the passion he had mistaken for love. Anyway, the love dissolved with startling rapidity, and in a half hour there was little tenderness remaining for the English girl who had repulsed him. He accepted her answer as conclusive, and began at once to revive his former plans of vengeance. One transport was liable to prove as sweet and exciting as another to him, and he began to revel in the consciousness that he was the supreme master of the fate of all the Consinors. Hatatcha was right after all. These English were cold and faithless, and unworthy the consideration of one of his noble race. He had been incautious and weak for a time, but now he resolved to fulfil his oath to the dead woman to the very letter.

He tore the offending paper into fragments, and left the room with a resumption of his old inscrutable demeanor. It was the look that Tadros had learned to fear.

"Drive me to the Savoy," he said to his chauffeur.

Lord Roane had reserved one small room on the first floor of the hotel as an office, and here he transacted such business matters as came under his jurisdiction. Kāra found him unoccupied, and Roane, who knew his visitor but slightly, greeted the man with cordial politeness.

"Pray be seated, Prince," said he, offering a chair; "I am entirely at your service."

The other bowed coldly.

"I fear my mission may prove somewhat disagreeable to you, my lord," he began, in quiet, even tones.

Roane gave him a shrewd glance.

"Ah, I hear that my son is largely indebted to you for losses in gambling," he returned, thinking that he understood Kāra's errand. "So far, it is merely a rumor that has reached me; but if you come to me to plead that case, I beg to assure you that I am in no way responsible for Consinor's debts of honor."

The Egyptian shrugged his shoulders as a Frenchman might have done.

"That is another matter, sir, which I do not care to discuss at this time," he answered. "My present business is to obtain your consent to marry your granddaughter."

Roane was startled with amazement.

"Aneth! You wish to marry Aneth?" he asked, as if he could not have heard aright.

"Yes, my lord."

So confident was the prince's tone that Lord Roane, although much unnerved by its suddenness, began involuntarily to consider the proposition. The fellow was handsome and dignified and reputed to be as rich as Crœsus; but the Englishman had a natural antipathy to foreigners, especially the dark-skinned ones. The idea of giving Aneth to an Egyptian was revolting.

"Ahem! This is indeed a surprise, Prince," he said, haltingly. "The child is hardly old enough yet to think of marriage."

Kāra did not reply to this observation.

"Have you—ah—approached her with this proposal as yet?" inquired Roane, after a few moments' reflection.

"I have, sir."

"And what did she say?"

"She refused to marry me, giving as her reason the fact that she does not love me," was the calm reply.

Roane stared at him.

"Then why the devil do you come to me?" he demanded, angrily.

"Because the girl must not be allowed to choose for herself," said Kāra.

"Must not, sir?"

"Decidedly not, Lord Roane. Too much depends upon her refusal. At present your granddaughter stands disgraced in the eyes of all the world, because of that dishonest father, who, as you remarked a moment ago, owes me ten thousand pounds."

"Aneth disgraced!" cried Roane, indignantly; "by no means, sir! Even your vile insinuations cannot injure that pure and innocent girl. But Consinor has gone away, and his daughter is now under my personal protection. I will see that she is accorded the respect and consideration to which she is entitled, despite her father's misdeeds."

"Such an assertion, my lord, is, under the circumstances, ridiculous," replied Kāra, with a composure equal to the other's irritation. "In the near future, when you are yourself disgraced and imprisoned, who will then be left to protect your granddaughter's good name?"

Roane uttered a roar of exasperation.

"You infernal scoundrel!" he exclaimed, "how dare you come here to browbeat and insult me! Leave my presence, sir!"

"I think you will be glad to hear more," remarked Kāra, without changing his position. "Perhaps you are not aware that your robbery of the Government through the contractor, McFarland, is fully known to me."

Roane fell back in his chair, white and trembling.

"It's a lie!" he muttered.

"It is not a lie," said the imperturbable Egyptian. "The proofs are all in my hands. I hold your receipt to McFarland for the stolen money."

Roane glared at him, but had not a word to reply. He felt like a rat in a trap. From the most unexpected source this blow had fallen upon him when least expected, and already he bitterly regretted his lapse from honesty.

"The Egyptian Government, when it learns the facts," continued Kāra, "will show you no mercy. Even Lord Cromer will insist upon your punishment, for he will resent any embezzlement in office that would bring the English colony here into disrepute. You must be aware of your danger without the necessity of my calling your attention to the fact; so that you have, absolutely, no hope of escape except through my clemency."

"What do you mean?" asked the old nobleman, hoarsely.

"That at present the secret is in my sole possession. It need never be disclosed. Give me Aneth in marriage, and you will not only secure your safety, but I will see that you want for nothing in the future. I am wealthy enough to promise this."

"The girl has refused you."

"Never mind. You will force her to accept me."

"No, by God, I will not!" cried Roane, springing to his feet. "Hell and all its imps shall not induce me to drag that innocent child to my own level. I am a felon because I am an ass, and an ass because I have no moral stamina; but even then, my heart is not as black as yours, Prince Kāra!"

The Egyptian listened unmoved.

"The matter deserves more careful consideration," said he. "Sentiment is very pretty when it does not conflict with personal safety. An examination of your case reveals comfort and prosperity on the one hand, disgrace and prison on the other."

"They weigh nothing against Aneth's happiness," returned the old man, promptly. "Expose me as soon as you like, sir, for nothing will ever induce me to save myself from the fruits of my folly at the expense of that poor girl. And now, go!"

Kāra smiled with quiet scorn.

"It is quite refreshing to witness your indignation," said he. "If it were equaled by your honesty, you would have no reason to fear me."

"Nor do I fear you now," retorted Lord Roane, defiantly. "Do your worst, you infamous nigger, for you cannot bribe me in anyway to abet your shameful proposals."

Kāra reddened at the epithet, but did not reply until he had risen and started to move toward the door. Then he half turned and said:

"It will enable you to appreciate your danger better, Lord Roane, if I tell you that I am but the instrument of an Egyptian woman named Hatatcha, whose life and happiness you once carelessly ruined. She did not forget, and her vengeance against you and yours will be terrible, believe me, unless you engage me to defeat it instead of accomplishing it. My personal interest induces me to bargain with you. What do you say, my lord? Shall we discuss this subject more fully, or do you wish me to go?"

Roane was staring at him with affrighted eyes. A thousand recollections flashed through his mind at the mention of Hatatcha's name, attended by a thousand terrors as he remembered his treatment of her. So lost was he in fear and wonder that Kāra had to speak again.

"Shall I go, my lord?"

"Yes," was the answer. It seemed to be wrenched from the old man's throbbing breast by a generosity that conquered his cowardice.

Kāra frowned. He was disappointed. But further argument was useless, and he went away, leaving Roane fairly stunned by the disclosures of the interview.

XVII

ANETH SURRENDERS

Kāra went straight to Aneth's apartments, insisting that he must see her.

The girl was much distressed by this sudden visit, and, thinking that the Egyptian wished merely to renew his protestations and appeals, tried hard to evade the ordeal of an interview. Mrs. Everingham was with her at the time, and in her perplexity Aneth confided to her in a few brief words Kāra's infatuation, and asked her advice how to act under such trying circumstances.

Mrs. Everingham was a woman of strong character and shrewd judgment. She was tall and admirably formed, with undoubted claims to beauty and a carriage queenly and dignified. The wife of a prominent engineer, she had lived much in the Orient and was accustomed to its unconventionalities as well as to its most representative social life. Although so much older than Aneth, the lady had manifested a fondness for the lonely girl from their first meeting, and had gladly taken her, as she expressed it, "under her wing," as well as to her sympathetic heart; so that Aneth had come to rely upon her friend in many ways, and now turned to her in this emergency.

"I think it will be best for you to see him," advised Mrs. Everingham, after a thoughtful consideration of the case. "If you evade the explanation he doubtless wishes to force upon you, he is the sort of man to annoy you persistently until you grant him an interview. Better have it over at once; and be positive with him, my dear, as well as gentle, so that you leave no hope alive to warrant his renewing his suit."

"Won't you stay with me, Lola?" begged Aneth.

"That would hardly be fair to Prince Kāra," smiled Mrs. Everingham, "for my presence would embarrass and humiliate him unnecessarily. No; I will withdraw into the next room, where I shall be within call, but invisible. Be brave, Aneth dear. These disagreeable duties are often thrust upon women who, like yourself, have a faculty of unconsciously winning men's hearts, and are exacted as inevitable penalties. I am sorry for the poor prince, but he is not of our race and had no business to fall in love with an English girl."

Then she kissed her protégé and retired to the adjoining room, taking pains to leave the door ajar. Aneth sighed, and called her Arab to admit Kāra.

When the Egyptian entered, his manner in no way indicated the despair of a rejected lover, or even the eagerness of one who hoped to successfully appeal his case. Instead, he bowed coldly, but with profound deference, and said:

"You must pardon me, Miss Aneth, for forcing this interview upon you; but it was necessary."

"Forgive me, also, Prince Kāra," faltered the girl. "I am sorry you came, for my answer was final. I can never—"

He waved his hand with a gesture of insolent indifference that arrested her words.

"You will not be called upon to repeat the dismissal conveyed in your letter," said he. "I may ask you to reverse your decision, but it will be a matter of business between us, in which inclination will have no part."

"Sir," she replied, shrinking back before his stern look, "I—I fear I do not understand you!"

"Be seated," he requested, "and I will explain."

She obeyed silently, with a partial recovery of her self-control. Strange as the Egyptian's words proved, they were, after all, more bearable than his endearing protestations would have been, and in her ignorance she welcomed any topic but love.

Kāra spoke with brutal frankness.

"The scandal caused by your father's dishonesty is too recent for you to have yet escaped its contamination," he began. "Lord Consinor has left Cairo owing me money, a matter of some ten thousand pounds. That you may have no cause to doubt my word, please to examine this note of hand. It is witnessed by two respectable gentlemen residing in this city."

He handed her the paper and she took it mechanically, wondering what it meant.

"According to our laws," he resumed, "I can bring an action to recover this money against any member of Consinor's family. I am assured such an action would ruin Lord Roane completely."

She was afraid of him now, but drew herself up proudly.

"That will not matter in the least, sir," she replied. "Lord Roane will gladly meet any just obligation, even though it may leave him penniless to do so."

"My lord does not express himself quite so honorably as that," replied Kāra, with an open sneer. "But this note of hand is really unimportant. I merely mentioned it to emphasize the debt that you and your grandfather already owe me. Your father has cleverly escaped the result of his misdeeds by absconding. Unfortunately, Lord Roane is unable to do the same thing."

"No one will blame Lord Roane for his son's faults," she protested, greatly distressed by the cruelty of Kāra's remarks.

"That is not my meaning," he replied. "Roane's own misdeeds are so much more serious than those of his son that, when they are discovered, he cannot escape a prison cell."

Aneth gasped in horror. The accusation was at first beyond belief; but Kāra's tone was positive and a sudden recollection of her grandfather's doubtful life flashed over her and made her dread to question further.

It was not needful. The man continued calmly to enlighten her concerning McFarland's crime and her grandfather's participation in it, while the girl sat with wide-open eyes and a look of despair upon her white face.

Finally Kāra produced a second paper.

"This, Miss Aneth," he said, more gently, "is the receipt signed by Lord Roane for his share of the stolen money. It is proof positive against him, and you will, of course, recognize his signature. Besides, I can produce two witnesses to the crime—a crime for which the penalty is, as I have hinted, a long term of imprisonment as well as dishonor through all the ages to come. But this is only for discovery. There is no penalty exacted for an undiscovered crime. Personally, I do not wish to see Lord Roane disgraced and sent to prison, or your invalid mother impoverished, and you, yourself, left to the mercies of a reproachful world; so I have come here today to save you all from these consequences of Roane's folly, if you will let me."

Aneth tried to control her bewilderment. She wanted to think calmly. So vividly had Kāra described Lord Roane's offense, that she saw it all before her as in a dream, and knew that the old man's feet were stumbling at the edge of a bottomless pit. But the last words of the Egyptian, if she heard them aright, seemed to promise a chance of her awakening and exorcising the nightmare.

"How can you save us?" she asked, wearily.

"By making you my wife," he answered. "It all rests with you, Miss Aneth. I alone can protect Lord Roane from any possibility of discovery, and I will do so if you now promise to marry me. More than that, I will pay off all the mortgages on your grandfather's estates, so that he may live in comfort during the remainder of his life, honored and respected by all. And you shall have your father's note of hand for the ten thousand pounds as soon as I receive your promise, as an earnest of my good faith."

"And if I refuse?" she suggested, trembling.

"Then you render me powerless to aid, and plunge your aged grandfather into prison, disgraced and humiliated beyond any hope of redemption."

"No, no! I cannot do that," she wailed, miserably. "He has been so good to me and loved me so fondly that I dare not—I will not—sacrifice him to secure my own happiness!"

"It is as I hoped," said Kāra, a note of triumph in his voice. "Do you promise, sacredly and on your honor, that you will marry me in return for my shielding your grandfather from the consequences of his crime?"

"Yes," she answered, clasping her hands with a shudder.

"And you will come to me any day and hour that I may appoint?"

"Yes."

"Aneth! Aneth! what have you said? What have you done?" cried Mrs. Everingham, running from her hiding-place to clasp the terrified girl in her arms.

"What have I done?" repeated Aneth, vacantly. "Why, Lola, I have saved my dear grandfather from disgrace and ruin."

"You shall not keep that promise!" declared the woman, turning fiercely to confront Kāra. "It was wrung from you by threats—by blackmail—and this scoundrel is playing upon your generous and loving heart. You shall never keep so absurd a promise."

"Yes," returned Aneth, bravely; "I have given my word, and I shall keep it."

Kāra laid a paper upon the table.

"There is your father's note, Miss Aneth. You may destroy it." He hesitated an instant, and then added the second paper. "And here is your grandfather's receipt for the stolen money. So fully do I trust to your good faith that I leave the incriminating evidence all in your own hands. Good afternoon, Miss Aneth."

With a bow, grave and courteous, he passed from the room, and Mrs. Everingham lifted the girl in her strong arms and carried her into the adjoining chamber to lay her tenderly upon her bed. The strain had been severe, and Aneth had fainted.

XVIII

Finding a Way

Gerald Winston endured several miserable, uneasy days following that of Lord Consinor's public disgrace. He longed to call upon Aneth, but dared not intrude, and so compromised by sending her a daily gift of flowers. At last, however, he decided to see Mrs. Everingham and endeavor to ascertain Aneth's condition, and whether her father's fault was making her as sorrowful as he feared.

He found Mrs. Everingham at her rooms in the Savoy, and was admitted at once.

"I want to ask you about Miss Consinor," he said, after he had been warmly greeted, for they were good friends and she was glad he had come.

"Aneth is very unhappy," was the sober reply.

"I can understand her humiliation, of course," he continued, with a sigh; "although I hoped she would be brave, and not take the unfortunate circumstance too much to heart."

"She is young," answered Mrs. Everingham, evasively, "and cannot view these things as composedly as we do. Moreover, you must remember that Lord Consinor's trouble touches her more deeply than anyone else."

"Unless it is the viscountess," he suggested.

"Oh, the poor viscountess knows nothing of it! She passes her time in an exclusive consideration of her own ailments, and will scarcely see her own daughter at all. Do you know, Gerald, I sometimes wonder how the child can be so sweet and womanly when her surroundings are so dreadful."

"I know what you mean," he said. "Consinor has always borne a doubtful reputation at home, and in past years Roane's life has also been more or less disgraceful. But the old fellow seems to be conducting himself very properly since he came to Egypt, and it is possible he has reformed his ways."

She did not reply at once, but sat musing until she asked, with startling abruptness:

"Gerald, do you love Aneth?"

He flushed and stammered in his endeavor to find words to reply. Since his interview with Kāra he had confessed to himself that he did love Aneth; but that another should discover his secret filled the big fellow with confusion.

"Why do you ask?" he faltered, to gain time.

"Because the girl needs true and loving friends more at this moment than in all her life to come," said she, earnestly.

"I will be her true friend in any event," he returned.

"But I must know more than that," persisted Mrs. Everingham. "Tell me frankly, Gerald, do you love her?"

"Yes."

"Well enough to wish to make her your wife, in spite of her family's shady history?"

"Yes," he said again, looking at her inquiringly.

"Then I shall confide to you a great secret; for it is right that you should be apprised of what is going on; and only you—with my assistance, to be sure—can hope to defeat the cunning plot that threatens to separate Aneth from you forever."

Thereupon she related to him the details of the interview she had overheard between Kāra and the girl, and told of the promise Aneth had made to save her grandfather from disgrace by marrying the Egyptian.

"But this is nonsense!" he exclaimed, angrily. "The man is a fool to wish to force any woman to marry him, and a scoundrel to use such means to accomplish his purpose."

"I know; I have discussed this matter with Aneth long and earnestly, but all in vain. She is determined to sacrifice herself to save Lord Roane from this disgrace; and Prince Kāra is inflexible. For some unknown reason he has determined to make this girl his wife, although he did not talk like a lover, and she told him frankly she could never love or even esteem him. Really, it seems incomprehensible."

"I know his reason well enough," answered Winston, moodily. "He is acting under the influence of the strongest and most evil human passion—revenge. If you will kindly listen, my friend, I will relate a bit of romance that should enable you to understand the Egyptian's purpose."

He proceeded to recount the story of Hatatcha and Lord Roane, adding his grounds for believing that Kāra had from the first contemplated the ruin of the entire Consinor family.

"This is horrible!" cried Mrs. Everingham, indignantly. "If what you say is true, this native prince is himself a grandson of Roane, and therefore Aneth's cousin."

"I have called his attention to that fact, and he declares it is no bar to his marrying her. I imagine his real meaning is that the relationship is no bar to his prosecuting his nefarious plans. Does Lord Roane know of this proposed sacrifice of his granddaughter for his sake?"

"No; and Aneth has made me promise to keep the secret from him. I cannot see that he would be able to assist us in anyway, if he knew all that we know."

"Perhaps not. Is the story true? Has Roane actually embezzled this money?"

"I do not know."

"It seems to me," said the young man, thoughtfully, "that our first action should be to discover the truth of Kāra's assertion. He may have trumped up the charge to work upon Aneth's feelings, and lead her to consent to marry him against her will."

"That is true," she said. "How can we investigate the matter?"

"Very easily. I will go tomorrow to the Rosetta Barrage and examine the embankment. Afterward I can look up the records and discover what sort of contract this man McFarland had, and how much money he collected for its execution. That will give us the truth of the matter, and I can accomplish it all in two days' time."

"Then go; but make haste, for everyday is precious. We do not know when the prince may call upon Aneth to fulfil her promise."

They discussed the situation a while longer, and then Winston withdrew to prepare for taking the early morning train.

The second evening after, he again called upon Mrs. Everingham.

"Well," she inquired, eagerly, "what did you discover?"

"It is all true," he answered, despondently. "The swindle has been cleverly consummated, and in just the way Kāra explained it to Aneth. There is no doubt of Lord Roane's guilt; neither can we doubt that Kāra has both the power and the will to expose and imprison him if it suits his purpose to do so."

"Then," said Mrs. Everingham, firmly, "we must find another way to save Aneth. The poor child is heart-broken, and moans every moment that she is left alone with her misery. Lord Roane tries earnestly to comfort her, for I am sure he loves her as well as one of his character is capable of loving. But he imagines she grieves over her father, and does not suspect the truth."

"Is she still resolved upon keeping her promise?" he inquired.

"Yes; and that in spite of all I can say to move her. The girl has a gentle and loving nature, but underneath it is a will of iron and a stubbornness such as the early martyrs must have possessed. She holds her own happiness as nothing when compared with her grandfather's safety."

"Then what can we do?" he asked, pacing the floor nervously.

"We must resort to a cunning equal to Kāra's in order to induce Aneth to break her foolish promise," responded Mrs. Everingham, promptly.

"I fear I do not quite understand," he said, stopping before her to read her countenance for the clue.

"I think—nay, Gerald, I am certain—the girl loves you; for I have questioned her skilfully during your absence and led her to speak of you, watching her tell-tale eyes as she did so. In my opinion it is this secret love for another that makes her sacrifice so grievous, and will end in breaking her heart."

He blushed like a girl at hearing this, but was evidently reassured and delighted.

"Yet I do not understand even now, Mrs. Everingham," he said.

"It is not so much that you are stupid as that you are a man," she answered, smiling. "You must become the instrument to save Aneth from herself. In a few moments I shall take you to see her. Her rooms are just across the hall, and doubtless she is at this moment alone, Lord Roane having left the hotel an hour ago. This evening I will give you countenance, but thereafter you must play your own game, and do your utmost to draw from Aneth a confession that she loves you. When you have done that, our case is won."

"Why so?"

"Can't you see, Gerald? No right-minded girl would ruin the life of the man she loves to save her grandfather from the consequences of his own errors. If she is in the mood to sacrifice, we will let her sacrifice Lord Roane instead of herself or you."

"Oh!" he said, blankly. "I can't do that, you know, Mrs. Everingham."

"Why not?"

"It would not be honest or fair. And it would be selfish in me, and—and unmanly."

"But I am not thinking of you at all, sir, except as the instrument. I am thinking of Aneth and her life's happiness. Are you willing, on your part, to sacrifice her to such a man as Kāra, that he may crush her to gratify his revenge?"

"No; but—"

"Will you permit her, in her blindness and folly, to break her own heart and ruin her own life, when you know that you can save her?"

"No."

"The struggle is between you and Kāra. Lord Roane is a felon, and to save him from the penalty due his acts will be to merely postpone the day when another of his criminal misdeeds will be discovered. There is little possible redemption for a man who has attained his sinful years; but if the possibility did exist, the price would be too high. Opposed to the desirability of shielding this reprobate nobleman and giving Kāra his way—which simply means Aneth's ruin—we must consider your mutual love and the prospect of a long life of happiness for you both. Do you dare to hesitate, Gerald Winston?"

"I will do exactly as you say, Mrs. Everingham," he replied, impetuously. "I can't let her go to this fiend—to the terrible fate that awaits her. Tell me what to do, and I will obey!"

"Your first duty will be to come with me to her room. And drop that long face, sir! Be cheery and lighthearted, and woo Aneth as tenderly as if you were wholly ignorant of the dreadful position she is in. Arrange to call again tomorrow, and in the future do not leave her alone for a single evening, and haunt her at all hours of the day. Remember that time is precious, and the situation demands all your skill and diplomacy. It cannot be a long siege; you must determine to capture her by attack."

"I—I'll try," he said, nervously.

And so he met Aneth again, for the first time since her trouble had come upon her, and he performed his part so creditably that Mrs. Everingham had but little fault to find with her coadjutor. The sight of the girl's swollen eyelids and her sad and resigned expression of countenance so aroused his loving pity and indignation at the cruel plot that had enmeshed her, that he could scarcely restrain the impulse to declare at once his love and entreat her to give him an immediate right to protect her.

Perhaps Aneth read something of his love for her in his eager face, for she joined with Mrs. Everingham in sustaining the flow of small talk that was likely to prove her best safeguard, and in this way was led to forget for the moment her cares and fears. She hesitated a moment when Gerald proposed to bring her a new book next afternoon, but finally consented. Therefore, he left her feeling more buoyant and hopeful than he had thought could be possible a few short hours before.

From that evening his former shyness disappeared, and he pushed his suit with as much ardor as he dared, utterly ignoring Aneth's evident desire to restrain him from speaking too plainly. But sometimes she, too, forgot her impending fate, and gave way to the delight of these happy moments. Already she knew that Gerald loved her, for her woman's instinct was alert, and at night she lay upon her bed and wailed miserably because the gates of paradise had suddenly opened before her, and her willing feet were so bound that she might not enter.

During these days Lord Roane devoted much of his time to his grandchild, treating her with almost reverential tenderness and striving in every possible way to cheer her spirits. The old man realized that his probation might be short. At any moment Kāra was liable to fulfil his threat and expose him to the authorities, and involuntarily he caught himself listening at all times for the footfall of the official coming to arrest him. He even wondered why he had escaped so long, knowing nothing of the manner in which Aneth had saved him.

And the girl, noting his loving care for her and marking the trouble that often clouded his handsome face, was encouraged in her resolve to carry out her compact with Kāra rather than see her aged grandfather thrust into prison, humiliated and disgraced.

Between her awakening love for Gerald Winston and her desire to save the family honor, the girl was indeed in pitiable straits. Yet never for a moment did she hesitate as to which way the path of duty led.

She felt that everyday she remained unmolested by the Egyptian was a precious boon to be grateful for, yet always she dreaded Kāra's summons. However, he was in no hurry, realizing the bitterness to her of these days of waiting, and enjoying the prolongation of her sufferings. All the love that Kāra had formerly borne the girl seemed to have dissolved as if by magic, and in its place had grown up schemes for so horrible a vengeance that he often wondered whether Hatatcha herself might not have hesitated to accomplish it.

But Kāra did not hesitate. The very diablerie of the thing fascinated and delighted him, and he anticipated the event with eager joy.

Tadros spent much of his time at the hotel, in charge of Kāra's elaborate system of espionage. His functions as dragoman gained for him special privileges, and the hall porter allowed him free access to the lobby; yet he was only able to enter the upper halls when he could plead some definite errand. This excuse was provided by a guest of the hotel, an agreeable Frenchman who was in Kāra's employ and maintained a surveillance over the interior of the establishment, while a half-dozen Arabs and Copts watched carefully the exterior. Thus Tadros was enabled to keep in close touch with the movements of Lord Roane and Aneth, as well as to spy upon those who might visit them, and his orders were to report promptly to Kāra any suspicious circumstances which might indicate that his victims were planning their escape.

But, from the dragoman's reports, all seemed well, and his prospective prey apparently made no effort to evade their fate.

Kāra depended much upon Aneth's delicate sense of honor and her strength of character, and read her so truly that there was little chance of her disappointing him. Roane, however, caused him a little uneasiness, and the Egyptian's spies shadowed him wherever he went. But Kāra misjudged the old gentleman if he supposed that Roane would tamely submit to Aneth's sacrifice had he known her secret. The girl understood him better, and although she did not know of his indignant rejection of Kāra's offer to shield him at the expense of his granddaughter's happiness, Aneth knew that if Roane learned the truth he would at once give himself up to justice in order to save her; and here was a danger the clever Egyptian had not even suspected.

In many of his dealings Roane was doubtless an unprincipled knave; but certain points of character were so impressed upon his nature, through inheritance from generations of more noble Consinors, that in matters of chivalry his honor could not be successfully challenged.

The dragoman said nothing to Kāra about Winston's frequent visits to Aneth. During his hours of watching Tadros indulged in reflection, and these musings encouraged a growing resentment toward his master that destroyed much of his value as a confidential servant. Aside from the resentment, Tadros was afraid of Kāra, and also uneasy as to his financial condition. The prince, who was accustomed to scatter money with a liberal hand, had of late refrained from exhibiting a single piastre. Tadros wondered, and grew suspicious. One evening, as he reported to Kāra, he said:

"The tradesmen are clamoring for their money. They say you are not paying them as promptly as you did heretofore."

Kāra looked up with surprise.

"Is not my credit good?" he inquired.

"For the present, yes," replied the dragoman; "but it will not remain good unless you begin to pay for all the magnificence you are putting into this villa."

"I see," said Kāra, nodding thoughtfully. "They are fools, my Tadros, but they might become troublesome. Keep them satisfied with promises for a time longer. That should not be a difficult task."

Tadros looked at him distrustfully.

"Tell me, my prince; have you spent all your treasure?" he asked.

The Egyptian smiled.

"If I should live a thousand years, my Tadros," he returned, "I could not spend the half of it."

"Then why do you not pay these merchants?"

"Because I have at this time no more money in the bank, and it is not convenient for me to leave Cairo just now to secure a further supply."

"Oh, I see!" remarked the dragoman, heaving a sigh of relief. "You must make another trip to Fedah."

Kāra gave him one of those intent, thoughtful looks that always made Tadros uneasy; but when he spoke his voice sounded soft and pleasant.

"What causes you to think my treasure is at Fedah, my good friend?" he asked.

The tone reassured the dragoman.

"It stands to reason, my prince, that it is there," he answered, with frank indifference. "Do I not well remember first seeing the papyri in your house, and afterward carrying away from there the heavy traveling case that was filled with precious gems?"

"Ah! was it?"

"Of course, Kāra. How else could you give so many ancient gems to the Van der Veens to recut, or turn so many more into money by selling them to Andalaft, the jeweler?"

"You have been observant, my Tadros."

"It is natural. I am no fool. But if, as you say, there is more treasure at Fedah, I will undertake to keep the rascally tradesmen quiet until you can make another deposit in the bank."

Kāra was still reading the countenance of his dragoman.

"It is quite evident that you are no fool, my Tadros," he said, softly; "yet I had not imagined you capable of so much shrewdness and wisdom. Look you! Fedah consists of a rock and a few stone houses cemented with Nile mud. It is familiar to you, being your birthplace as well as my own. Now where do you suppose, within the limits of that simple village, a treasure could have been discovered?"

"It has puzzled me," acknowledged Tadros; "but I suppose you do not wish me to know the exact location. Nevertheless, it is evident that the treasure is a very ancient one, and therefore it must have been hidden by your forefathers in the mountain itself, or perhaps on the desert that adjoins the village."

"A long-buried and forgotten temple; eh, Tadros?"

"Oh, no; a tomb, of course! They did not keep pearls and rubies in the temples. Only in tombs could such trinkets be found. That is why I believe your statement that you are the last descendant of the great kings of Egypt; for this tomb was not discovered by accident, I know. The secret of its existence must have been handed down through the generations. Hatatcha knew, and told you of it before she died; so it is your personal property, and its possession proves your noble blood. I am glad the treasure is ample; for at the rate you are squandering money, it would otherwise be soon exhausted."

"Very wisely argued, indeed," said Kāra. "I wonder how much of my inheritance has already found its way into your own pockets."

"Not too much, you may be sure," answered the dragoman, gravely. "I am very honest, and take only my rightful perquisites. It is better that these trifles should go to me than to strangers, for I am your own kinsman and almost as pure an Egyptian as yourself."

"True. I do not complain, my Tadros. But in acquiring my money you should take care not to acquire too much knowledge of my affairs with it, for such knowledge is liable to prove extremely dangerous. Consider the pearls of wisdom that have even now dropped from your lips. Must they not be repaid? And already I am greatly in your debt."

"You are talking riddles," growled the dragoman, uneasily. "Tell me what you mean in plain words."

"Do you remember the day that Nephthys broke her water-jar?"

"Yes."

"You struck me, your prince, and knocked me down."

"Well, you choked me afterward. That should even the score."

"Not quite. I choked you for spying upon me. That was another offense. The blow has not yet been accounted for."

Tadros frowned.

"I do not bear grudges myself," he muttered.

"There are a few other matters scored against your account," continued Kāra. "Still, so long as you serve me faithfully, and I have need of you, I shall not exact a reckoning; but they stand on record, my Tadros, and some day the account must be balanced. Do not forget that. For these reasons, and remembering that you have declared yourself no fool, I am certain that you will admit you were wrong about the location of my treasure. When you think it over, you will conclude that it lies in Luxor, or Abydos, or perhaps is a myth altogether, and never has existed. And, when you chatter to others, no mention of a hidden tomb or temple will be permitted to pass your lips. I am quite sure you will be circumspect, and I trust you to keep to yourself the secret of my affairs. If I thought you would betray me, I would kill you now, instead of waiting. But you will not do that; you are too fond of living and of the money you are saving to hazard losing both."

Tadros returned to his duties in a very thoughtful mood. In playing upon his fears, Kāra had overreached himself, and made the dragoman so much afraid that he believed his life hung by a thread. Therefore, he sought most earnestly for a way of escape from the thrall of his terrible countryman.

The following morning Gerald Winston, on leaving Mrs. Everingham after a conference concerning their plans, met Tadros face to face in the corridor of the hotel. He recognized the man at once as Kāra's dragoman and confidential servant. Moreover, he suspected that the fellow had just come from the Consinor apartments; so he had no hesitation in accosting him.

"May I speak with you a moment in private?" he asked.

"Most certainly, sir."

Winston led the way into Mrs. Everingham's drawing-room, where the lady greeted his return with surprise, but a quick appreciation of the importance of securing an interview with Kāra's confidant.

"You are Prince Kāra's dragoman, I believe?" began the Englishman.

"Yes, Winston Bey."

"And devoted to him personally, of course?"

"To an extent, naturally," returned Tadros, hesitating what to say. "You see, he pays me liberally."

Winston and Mrs. Everingham exchanged glances. Then the lady took up the conversation.

"Prince Kāra," she said, in a stern tone, "is a scoundrel, being even now engaged in perfecting one of the most diabolical plots the mind of man has ever conceived."

Tadros did not reply. It was not his business to deny the charge.

"Our desire and intention to defeat this plot," she continued, "lead us to speak to you frankly. We must save Miss Consinor from an ignoble alliance with your master."

Tadros listened carefully.

"To accomplish our purpose, we are willing to expend a great deal of money—enough to make some faithful ally comfortable for the remainder of his life."

A pause followed this significant statement. Tadros felt the effect of their scrutinizing glances, and cleared his throat while he looked swiftly around to make sure they could not be overheard. Then, reassured, he answered with his native bluntness of speech.

"I am willing to earn this money," said he, "if you will show me how to do it with safety. Kāra is a fiend. He would not hesitate to kill all three of us if he had reason to suspect we were plotting against him."

"I will give you a thousand pounds," said Winston, "if you will tell us what you know of Kāra's plans. I will give you two thousand pounds additional if we succeed in saving Miss Consinor."

Tadros was pleased. He had intended to break with Kāra anyway. To be well paid for doing this was a stroke of good fortune.

"I accept your offer," he replied. "But I must inform you that there is no time to be lost. I have just taken a message to Miss Consinor, telling her to be ready to go to Kāra at nine o'clock this evening."

"This evening!" exclaimed Winston, alarmed. "And what was her reply?"

"She assured me that she would keep her compact with the prince and be ready to accompany me at the hour named. I am to call for her and take her in a closed carriage to Kāra's villa."

"And then?" asked Mrs. Everingham, eagerly.

"Then there is to be a mock ceremony of marriage, which is intended to entrap the young lady so that she will think everything is regular, and will make no disturbance," answered Tadros, calmly. "A Copt, named Mykel, who is one of Kāra's servants, is to be dressed as a priest and perform the Coptic marriage service, which is a Christian function not unlike your own. But the man is not a priest, and the marriage will be illegal. The intention is to destroy the young lady's good name, after which Kāra will drive her away. Then he intends to deliver her grandfather, Lord Roane, over to justice."

"What a dreadful crime!" exclaimed Mrs. Everingham, indignantly. "And Aneth is sacrificing herself because she believes the act will save her grandfather."

"That is Kāra's promise," returned the dragoman. "But he has no intention of keeping it. Did he not give her a forged copy of Roane's receipt? For some reason my prince aims at the ruin of the entire Consinor family. The young lady's father he has already disgraced and driven from Cairo."

"I understand his motive," said Winston, "and believe you are right in claiming that Kāra will not spare Lord Roane once Aneth is in his power. The danger is terrible and imminent, for nothing will move Aneth to abandon her purpose. She imagines she is saving Roane, and has exacted from us a promise not to tell the old gentleman of her sacrifice. So our hands are tied."

"It seems to me," declared Mrs. Everingham, after a moment's thought, "that we must use the self-same weapons in fighting Kāra that he is employing. With the dragoman's assistance it ought to be easy to save Aneth, even against her will."

"In what way?" inquired Gerald, earnestly.

She did not reply at once. Instead, she studied the dragoman's countenance with steadfast eyes.

"What is your name?" she asked.

"Tadros, madam."

"Will you follow our instructions faithfully, and not betray us to Prince Kāra?"

"Yes. I hate Kāra. He will kill me for deserting him if he gets the chance; but then he intends to kill me anyway as soon as he can spare my services. If your plan includes the murder of Prince Kāra, I shall be very glad."

"It does not; but we will protect you from any harm, rest assured. Your task is simple. When you call for Miss Consinor tonight you will drive her, not to the prince's villa, but to the embankment, where you will place her on board Winston Bey's dahabeah. It will lie opposite Roda, on the west bank. Cross the Gizireh bridge and drive as rapidly as possible to the boat, where we shall be waiting to receive you."

"My dahabeah!" cried Winston, astonished.

"To be sure. You will have everything in readiness for a voyage up the Nile, with a prisoner aboard."

"A prisoner?"

"Yes; Aneth. She will, of course, refuse to go willingly, having given Kāra her word. I will accompany the party as her keeper, and we must find some way to induce Lord Roane to join us also. Once afloat on the mysterious river, Kāra will have no means of knowing what has become of his victims, and before we return, my friend, we shall have perfected such arrangements as will render the prince's intention to marry our Aneth impossible. That is why I desire Lord Roane to join the party. He also will be safe from Kāra for a time."

"I understand you now," said Winston; "and while I do not see quite to the end of the adventure, the plan will at least give us time to formulate our future action and enable us to thwart Kāra's immediate schemes."

"That is my idea," she returned. "Something must be done at once; and by abducting Aneth, we not only gain time, but save her temporarily from the consequences of her own folly."

Then she turned to Tadros.

"What do you think of my plan?" she asked.

"It is excellent," said he, "except for one thing; there are several spies about this hotel, who would at once follow us and inform Kāra that we had boarded the dahabeah; but I think I can find a way to throw them off the scent. They are under my orders, and I will send them to other stations before nine o'clock. Aside from this, then, do I understand that my only duty is to deliver the young lady on board the dahabeah?"

"That is all we ask."

"I will show three red lights," said Winston, "so that you cannot mistake the exact location of the boat."

"I know the boat," replied the dragoman. "Abdallah, your engineer, is a friend of mine."

"You will not fail us?" asked Mrs. Everingham, anxiously. "All depends upon you, Tadros!"

"I know, and I will not fail you," he said.

"I believe you will earn the three thousand pounds," remarked Winston, significantly.

"As for that, sir," replied the dragoman, with dignity, "I hope you will give me credit for a little humanity as well as cupidity. Being an Egyptian, I love money; being a man, I am eager to assist a woman in distress. But, above all else, I shall have pleasure in defying Kāra, who hates me as heartily as I hate him. Thus, three passions vouch for my fidelity—love, pity and hatred. Can you doubt my devotion to the cause?"

After this he went away, leaving his fellow-conspirators to plan the details of the evening's adventure.

XIX

The Abduction

Mrs. Everingham passed the afternoon in Aneth's company. The girl was visibly nervous and excited, but made pitiful attempts to conceal her weakness. In no way did she allude to Kāra or to the fact that the hour had arrived when she was to consummate the sacrifice of her own happiness to maintain her grandfather's integrity and the honor of her family's name.

Her friend ventured one or two remarks about the folly of her promise and the absurdity of keeping it; but these so distressed Aneth, and had so little visible influence upon her decision, that Mrs. Everingham abandoned the topic and turned the conversation into more cheerful channels. When she mentioned Gerald Winston she noticed that Aneth's cheeks flamed scarlet and then turned deathly white; so here was another subject to be avoided, if she did not wish to make the girl's position unbearable. Indeed, those last days of association with Gerald had taught Aneth the full extent of her martyrdom, and now she began to realize that she was losing all that might have rendered her life's happiness complete, had it not been for the advent of Kāra and his terrible threat to destroy the family honor and send her loving grandfather to prison.

Early in the evening Mrs. Everingham kissed her friend and returned to her own room across the corridor, there to complete her simple preparations for the proposed voyage.

Meantime Winston had been busy with Lord Roane. The young man was fortunately a prime favorite with Aneth's grandsire, and he listened attentively to Gerald's explanation of a plot to rescue his darling grandchild from the slough of despondency into which she had fallen.

"Mrs. Everingham is confident a Nile voyage would do much to cheer her up and keep her from dwelling upon her troubles," he suggested. "What do you think of the idea, sir?"

"Capital," said Roane—"if Aneth can be induced to consent. I asked her to run over to Helwan the other day, for a few weeks' change of scene; but she declared she would not listen to such a proposal."

"That is our difficulty," acknowledged Winston, speaking in a confidential tone. "She has told Mrs. Everingham she would not leave Cairo, but we think her decision is based upon the fear that you would be unable to accompany her; so we have decided to engage in a little conspiracy, for the morbid condition into which she has fallen has made us all anxious. Is there any reason, my lord, why you should not leave Cairo for a month or so?"

"None whatever, if my going will benefit Aneth in anyway."

"Very good! Now, here is our plan. I have fitted my private dahabeah for a cruise. Mrs. Everingham will go along to chaperone your granddaughter, and you will join us to complete her happiness and keep her contented. Only one thing stands in our way—the young lady's refusal to embark. That barrier will be surmounted by Mrs. Everingham, who is a woman of experience and who loves Aneth as well as if she were her own daughter. So this evening you and I will get aboard quietly, without declaring our intentions to anyone, and rely upon Mrs. Everingham's promise to join us with Aneth at nine o'clock. Do not ask me, sir, how she will succeed in overcoming your granddaughter's scruples against leaving Cairo. We will trust to woman's wit. When the party is embarked, we go up the Nile, to find roses for your grandchild's pale cheeks and have a jolly good time as well."

Roane accepted the program with enthusiasm. He himself was in a dreadfully nervous state, expecting hourly to be accused of a crime the proof of which would separate him forever from Aneth. To get away from Cairo just now, without Kāra's knowing where he had gone, would be to gain a few weeks' respite. Eagerly he availed himself of the opportunity.

Winston knew there was no danger of the old man's betraying their plans, but he could not divine what Kāra's next move might be, and resolved to take no chances; so he clung fast to Roane until he had put him and his light luggage aboard the dahabeah, whereupon he sent a messenger to apprise Mrs. Everingham of his success.

So far, all had gone well; but Mrs. Everingham's anxiety grew as the hour of nine approached. Lord Roane had sent word to Aneth that he would be out for dinner and might not return to the hotel until late that night; so the girl, glad of this fortunate chance, had her dinner served in her own room, and the Arab servant, being intercepted by Mrs. Everingham, declared that she ate little and wept continually, as if overcome by some hopeless sorrow.

All depended now upon the faithfulness of Tadros the dragoman, and Mrs. Everingham, finding nothing more for her woman's ingenuity to devise, entered a carriage at half past-eight o'clock and was driven quietly to the embankment. Within sight of the three red lights Winston had displayed, she halted her vehicle to await the arrival of the dragoman.

Tadros, meantime, being fully instructed by Kāra as to the conduct of his mission, drove in the Egyptian's private carriage to the hotel. The coachman had been instructed to obey the dragoman's orders implicitly, so he suspected nothing when Tadros, having alighted at the Savoy, commanded him to drive to the citadel and remain in the shadow of the mosque until midnight.

The dragoman then hired another carriage that was driven by a sleepy and stupid-looking Arab, after which he immediately entered the hotel and went directly to Aneth's room.

She opened the door in person, having dismissed all her attendants.

"It is nine o'clock, miss," announced Tadros, as he entered.

The girl clasped her hands with a gesture and look of terror.

"Where is—is—Prince Kāra?" she asked, vaguely.

"At his villa, awaiting, with the bridal party, your arrival. You must understand that the wedding is to be very quietly conducted, yet strictly in accordance with the requirements of the Christian faith. My master desires me to say that every consideration and courtesy shall be shown you, his highest ambition in the future being to promote your happiness."

She shuddered.

"Is that all he said?"

"Except that his promises to you shall be faithfully kept, and Lord Roane's comfort and safety carefully provided for."

"Let us go," she said, hastily. "I am ready."

"Any luggage, miss?" he asked.

She pointed to a small traveling-case that stood beside her, and Tadros stooped and picked it up.

With a frightened glance around her, she placed a note directed to Lord Roane upon the table and then hurriedly left the room, leaving the door unlocked.

The dragoman escorted her to the side entrance, reserved for ladies, and they were fortunate in finding it almost deserted at that moment. Aneth entered the carriage quickly, as if fearful of being interrupted in her escape, and Tadros closed the door and took his seat beside the driver.

"To the opera house," he said, for the benefit of the few loungers who stood upon the pavement.

After driving a couple of blocks, he made the Arab driver stop in front of a tobacco shop, and sent him in to purchase some cigarettes. The moment the fellow disappeared, Tadros started the horse and applied the whip, and the carriage had whirled swiftly around the corner before the wondering Arab returned to the street, to find his equipage and his passengers missing.

Aneth, as soon as she had leaned back against the cushions, had fallen into a sort of stupor. Her weary brain refused to think or to speculate upon the doubtful fate to which she was rushing. She felt the carriage bumping over the crossings and saw vaguely the lights flash by; but she noted neither the direction in which they were proceeding nor the length of their journey. Across the Nile bridge the horses abated their speed; but then through the darker lanes of the west embankment they dashed along at a wild pace, that might have frightened the girl, had she been capable of realizing the actual conditions.

Suddenly, with a jolt that almost threw her into the opposite seat, the carriage halted. She looked out of the window and saw three dim red lights burning, and beyond these the glint of a stray moonbeam upon the river.

When Tadros came to assist her in alighting, she saw Mrs. Everingham standing behind him.

"Where am I?" asked the girl, wildly.

"Hush, dear," said her friend, taking her in her arms to kiss her tenderly. "Am I not welcome at your wedding?"

"But why are we here?" asked Aneth, pleadingly. "Why are we at the river, and where is Prince Kāra?"

"Come and let me surprise you," answered Mrs. Everingham, soothingly, leading the young girl, who was still half dazed and thoroughly mystified, aboard the dahabeah and into the brightly lighted little cabin. There sat Lord Roane and Gerald Winston.

Aneth stared, and then, looking wildly around, she gave a plaintive cry and threw herself into her grandfather's arms.

"I don't understand!" she wailed, sobbing hysterically. "What does it all mean? Why are you here, and where is Prince Kāra?"

Roane was puzzled by her speech, as well as distressed by her agitation.

"Prince Kāra!" he repeated. "Confound it, Aneth, you don't want that rascally nigger, do you?"

"No, no!" she replied; "but he wants me, and I have promised; I must go to him. Why am I here? What have you done?"

By this time the dragoman had tied his horses to a palm and come aboard, just as Hassan drew in the gangplank and Abdallah started the wheezy engine. Tadros stood in the cabin doorway and listened intently to Aneth's protests.

"See here, miss," he exclaimed, with assumed sternness, "you are in my charge, for I am Prince Kāra's dragoman, and you have promised to obey me. Is it not so?"

She turned to look at him.

"Are you obeying Prince Kāra's orders?" she demanded.

"To be sure! He wished to surprise you. He says he merely intended to test your honesty, being interested in knowing whether an English girl would keep her promises. But he does not desire to make you unhappy. He is a prince, and generous; therefore, he releases you from your compact, and you are free from this time forth to do exactly as you please."

She was white and trembling now.

"But my grandfather—" she began, eagerly.

Tadros cut her short.

"He also is safe, in proof of which you see him at your side. You need have no fears in the future that—"

He stopped abruptly, for the overwrought nerves of the girl could not withstand this sudden revulsion of fate. Gerald caught her swaying form and carried her to her berth, where Mrs. Everingham tended her lovingly and applied restoratives to relieve her faintness.

As for Lord Roane, he swore loudly and glared upon the dragoman.

"What cursed nonsense is this?" he cried.

Tadros smiled, and Gerald came up and seized the dragoman by both hands, pressing them warmly.

"Thank you, my man!" said he. "You are a loyal ally, and I shall not forget how you have lied to save us from an embarrassing position." Then he turned to Lord Roane. "If there is anything your lordship does not understand," he said, "I will gladly endeavor to explain it. Prince Kāra has been playing a deep game, with you and Aneth as pawns; but I think we have him checkmated at last."

The old nobleman did not reply at once. Any questioning on his part would necessarily be a very delicate matter. He turned his eyes thoughtfully toward the shore, where the lights of Cairo were slowly disappearing from their view.

XX

The Sheik Agrees

Kāra congratulated himself. For one whose early life had been passed in a hovel, he had been very successful in directing the destinies of the great. All his grandmother's vengeful plans, supplemented by his own clever arrangement of details, had matured in a remarkably satisfactory manner, and this evening he was destined to complete the ruin of Lord Roane's family. In addition to compromising Aneth beyond all hope by a false marriage, he would tomorrow have my lord cast into prison on a charge of embezzlement. The proof which he had pretended to place in the girl's keeping, and which she had without doubt promptly destroyed, was merely a forgery of the receipt to McFarland. The original was still safe in his custody.

This ruse had been a clever one. His judgment of the girl's nature was marvelously accurate. Having destroyed the paper to insure her grandfather's safety, Aneth was effectually prevented from breaking her contract with Kāra. There was no way for her to recede. He had paid the price, and she was left with no excuse for not fulfilling her part of the agreement.

When Kāra entered his courtyard he found it ablaze with lights. The women's apartments, now completely refitted, were truly magnificent. A dozen servants, arrayed in splendid costumes, stood motionless at their posts, awaiting the arrival of their new mistress. Mykel, a rascally Copt whom Kāra had recently attached to his household, was clad in priestly robes, and paced up and down the court with an assumed dignity that elicited sly smiles from his fellow-servants.

Only the prince's own people were present, for Kāra wished to be in a position to deny even the farce of a ceremony, should Aneth attempt in the future to use it as an excuse for her downfall. But it pleased him to lull her suspicions in this way in the beginning, and so render her an easy victim. It also gave an added flavor to his revenge.

Tadros had been carefully instructed, and would have no difficulty in fulfilling his mission. He ought to reach the villa on his return by half-past nine, allowing for natural delays. Kāra trusted Tadros because the dragoman was so completely in his power; but, with his usual caution, he had sent a spy to watch his messenger and report any irregularity in his conduct. Tadros did not know of this spy; otherwise, he might have felt less confidence in himself.

Half-past nine arrived, but no sound of carriage wheels broke the stillness. The servants stood motionless in their places, and Kāra paced the courtyard in deep reflection while engaged in drawing on his white kid gloves. The false priest stood under the bower of roses where the ceremony was to take place, trying to find the service in the Coptic Bible he had borrowed.

Nine-forty-five; ten o'clock. The dark-eyed servants noticed that their master grew uneasy and cast anxious glances toward the entrance.

It was twenty minutes later, when the nerves of the most unconcerned were beginning to get on edge, that the patter of horses' feet and the rapid whir of wheels broke the silence. A carriage dashed up to the villa and halted.

Kāra hurried forward expectantly, but paused abruptly when he met the spy who had been sent to watch Tadros.

"Where is the dragoman?" he demanded, in a sharp voice.

"The dragoman, your highness, is a traitor," said the man.

Kāra's nervousness suddenly subsided. He became composed in demeanor and his voice grew soft.

"Explain, if you please," said he.

The man bowed.

"Arriving at the hotel, Tadros sent away your excellency's carriage—"

"Where is it now?"

"I do not know. Then he engaged another equipage—that of the Arab named Effta Marada, bearing the number of ninety-three. Tadros brought the young lady down and placed her in Effta's carriage, ordering him to drive to the opera house. I sprang up behind and accompanied them. Tadros soon got rid of Effta by sending him on an errand and then drove quickly away. He crossed the Nile to the west embankment and drove down the river to a point opposite the island of Roda, where your dragoman placed the lady on board a dahabeah."

"Yes; go on."

"When the boat steamed away up the river, I took the deserted carriage and drove here as rapidly as possible. That is all, your excellency."

"Whose dahabeah was it?"

"That belonging to Winston Bey. I saw him on board."

"Did you see anyone else?"

"The lady who has been a friend to Miss Consinor."

"That is Mrs. Everingham."

"And an old Englishman, Lord Roane."

"Ah! Quite a family party. And our dear Tadros went with them?"

"He did, your excellency."

"Up the river, you say?"

"Yes, your excellency."

"Thank you. You may retire."

Kāra turned to Ebbek.

"Put out the lights and send the servants to their quarters," he said, calmly.

In his room the prince tore off the white gloves and changed from evening dress to a gray traveling suit. Then he returned to the now deserted courtyard and sat down in the moonlight beside the fountain to smoke a cigar.

The blow had been sharp and sudden. While Kāra fully realized the natural capability of Tadros for deception and double dealing, he also knew that the blustering dragoman was an arrant coward, and so was bewildered at the courage manifested in his treachery.

But it was characteristic of Kāra that he neither bemoaned his adverse fortune nor became despondent. He entertained a passing regret that he had delayed killing the dragoman, but did not permit himself to dwell long upon his servant's defection. The thing to be first sought was a remedy for the apparent failure of his carefully laid plans. By and by he would attend to the dragoman's reward. Just now it was imperative to prevent his intended victims from succeeding in their attempt to escape.

There was no demand for immediate action. The dahabeah was, as he knew, a slow steamer, and would be forced to breast the Nile current sluggishly. His enemies doubtless depended for their safety from pursuit upon Kāra's supposed ignorance of their whereabouts. He admitted that someone had plotted shrewdly against him. On the Nile a party in a small boat is almost as isolated as if at sea. The express steamers and tourist steamers pass now and then, but they travel rapidly, appearing and disappearing within the brief space of half an hour. Aside from these, only the native barges, picturesque and ghostlike as they drift by, break the ripples of the broad river. The banks are sprinkled with many villages, and at this season shaduf workers are plentiful; but the native has tired of staring at the Nile flotilla, unless awaiting with eagerness the landing of the big tourist steamer, from whose passengers a scant livelihood is gained, and this occurs only at certain points of interest.

So Kāra had time to be deliberate. It even occurred to him that this seeming calamity might turn out to be exceptionally favorable to the success of his schemes. In Cairo one must act with circumspection, because the police of the city are alert and almost incorruptible. The Nile dwellers fear the law rather than respect it; but they are too far from the capital to be very much afraid. Where tourists disembark, a mounted officer is stationed to lash the impudent villagers into a state of dull apathy, such as the caged tiger feels for its trainer; but they lapse into savagery when his back is turned, and in the more unfrequented villages the sheik is absolute king.

Kāra considered carefully these conditions, and soon formed new plans to complete his vengeance. Then, the cigar being finished, he went to bed and slept until daybreak.

"I shall be absent for several days," he said to Ebbek, as he ate an early breakfast. "See that everything is in perfect order when I return. If tradesmen come to demand money, promise them payment immediately on my arrival in Cairo."

"Yes, my master."

He caught the morning train for Luxor and arrived by noon at a station opposite the native village of Beni-Hassan, whence he crossed the river in a small boat.

The children of Hassan have for centuries been known as "the bandits of the Nile," and their three connected villages, lying close to the river bank, have replaced those that were totally destroyed by the Government during the reign of Mohammed 'Ali in the hope of scattering the tribes and breaking up their thieving propensities; but the Beni-Hassans rebuilt their mud dwellings and calmly remained in possession. Today they are cautiously avoided by isolated tourists, who are fully warned of their evil reputation.

As he landed, Kāra found the villages seemingly deserted. Underneath the tall palms at the right a few swathed figures lay motionless, while small black goats and stray chickens wandered listlessly about; but the visitor paid little attention to these signs. He knew the old men and women were swarming in the huts while the younger men were away at the distant tombs in the hills or engaged in earning a stipend at the neighboring shadufs.

Turning to the left, he followed a path leading up a slight incline to the low bluff covered with a second grove of stately palms, beneath the shade of which the better dwellings of Beni-Hassan have been built. He had never been in the village before, but had heard it described innumerable times since his boyhood. Even when he paused before an extensive building having cane and mud walls and a roof of palm leaves, he was fairly certain he had correctly guessed the location of the place he sought.

"Does Sheik Antar live here?" he asked a child that came out to stare at him.

The little one nodded and ran within. Kāra sat down cross-legged upon the path of baked mud, removed both his shoes and placed them beside him, and then patiently awaited his reception.

After some five minutes a gigantic Arab bent his head to emerge from the low doorway, and, after a calm but shrewd glance at his visitor, came forward and stood before Kāra.

"Allahu akbar!" he said, spreading wide his arms in greeting. "The stranger is welcome to all that I possess."

"May Allah bless and guard the habitation of the mighty sheik!" responded Kāra, in purest Arabic.

Then the sheik sat cross-legged upon the ground, facing his guest, and also removed his red morocco slippers. His beard was gray and his eyes black and piercing. His frame was lean and the flesh hard as iron, denoting great strength. He wore the green turban that proved he had made the Mecca pilgrimage.

"It pleases me that I behold the mighty Sheik Antar, beloved of Allah, and the curse of all enemies of the prophet," began Kāra after a brief silence, during which the men eyed each other earnestly.

"My brother speaks well," was the grave reply; "yet so lost am I in wonder at the glory and honor conferred upon my humble home by his presence, that the exalted name of my guest escapes my fickle memory."

Kāra bowed to the ground.

"I am of Gebel Abu Fedah, the grandson of the Princess Hatatcha, and descended from the line of Ahtka-Rā and the royal kings of ancient Egypt. My name is Kāra."

With dignified gesture the sheik extended his hand and clasped that of the stranger.

"The fame of the last great Egyptian has already reached my ears," said he. "Raschid, the Syrian dragoman, whose boat, the *Rameses*, was here but three days since, told me of your life in Cairo, of your magnificence and vast riches, of your generosity and wisdom. Fedah I know, for the sheik of Al-Kusiyeh is my comrade. The glory of Kāra the Egyptian is reflected upon every dweller along the Nile bank."

After another pause to permit of due and deliberate appreciation of this compliment, Kāra drew a heavy sigh and responded:

"Yet all is not at peace with me, most noble Antar. My enemies oppress me and cause me much sorrow; wherefore I am driven to appeal to my brother for aid."

The eyes of the sheik sparkled.

"Already," said he, "confusion has fallen upon Kāra's foes; for they surely cannot escape the blight of Antar's hatred!"

"Then see how gratitude flows from my heart like a very cataract," answered the other, with downcast eyes. "It is little that Kāra can do to repay such brotherly love; but the great sheik must distribute for me ten thousand piastres to his worthy poor, even on that day when my enemies are confounded."

Antar's brow was thoughtful. A great payment meant a great service.

"My brother will tell me a story," said he, "and I will listen."

Thereupon, in the flowery language of Arabia, which English words but feebly translate, the Egyptian told of a boat steaming slowly up the Nile and bearing his enemies toward the villages of Beni-Hassan. He described the women and the men, and noticed that the sheik grunted with discouraging emphasis when Winston Bey's name was mentioned. Then, following out the idea of relating a tale, Kāra told how his brother, the mighty sheik Antar, fell upon the dahabeah and captured it, turning over all the passengers and crew to Kāra except one—Tadros the dragoman being unfortunately killed and dropped overboard to find a final resting-place in the mud at the river's bottom. Then Winston's crew was replaced by six strong men of Beni-Hassan, who obeyed Kāra's commands as willingly as if they proceeded from Antar himself. And Kāra afterward steamed up the Nile to Fedah, with the sheik on board, and at Fedah gave to him not only the ten thousand piastres for his poor, but many gems of fabulous worth for his personal adornment and that of his women.

Was it not a pretty story? he concluded, and did it not sound like a prophecy in Antar's discerning ears?

The sheik considered long and earnestly. He did not like meddling with Winston Bey, whom he knew of old and respected highly; but

Kāra's allusion to the gems was irresistible, and Antar might discover a way to keep from being recognized by the scientist.

It required several hours to conclude the bargain, but at last both men thoroughly understood the details of the service that was required and must be rendered. The assault upon the dahabeah was discussed and planned, and the terms of payment agreed upon. The killing of Tadros was an incident that the sheik accepted without demur.

With two clever rascals such as the Egyptian and the Arab in charge of the raid, there seemed little hope that Winston Bey's unsuspecting party could escape absolute destruction.

XXI

Lotus-Eaters and Crocodiles

I f in all the realm of travel there is a voyage that is absolutely ideal, it is the trip up the Nile. The constant change of scene, varying with every bend in the river; the shifting lights, the gentle ripple of the waters, the distant songs and shouts of the native boatmen; the outlines of the Libyan hills by moonlight and the rocky wastes of desert, dotted with gorgeous crimson and yellow cacti, by day; the sunsets that paint the cloudless Egyptian skies with entrancing splendor, and the silhouettes of donkey and camel trains above the high embankment at twilight; these, taken in connection with the care-free, lotus-eating existence of the voyager, leave an impression so vivid and sweet and altogether satisfactory that no other experience in the whole world of travel can compare with or ever efface it from one's memory.

Aneth believed the dragoman's assertion that Prince Kāra had been generous at last and released her from her promise. Neither Winston nor Mrs. Everingham dared vouch for the dragoman's statements; but they remained silent while Tadros, unabashed, explained that his master was whimsical and erratic, but very kind-hearted and considerate, and incapable of wronging anyone in anyway.

"As for Lord Roane, miss," he said, confidentially, "there is no doubt he did an imprudent thing, which vexed my master, who has a high sense of honor; so he frightened my lord, to teach him to be more careful in the future. But never had he the slightest idea of exposing him to public infamy, I assure you. Kāra has told me so himself."

The dragoman derived much satisfaction from these inventions, especially as he noticed how implicitly Aneth believed them, and how they operated to cheer her spirits and render her content with her novel and delightful surroundings. Everyone on board was devoted to the girl, and, under the genial influences of the voyage, she recovered, to an extent, her old brightness and vivacity. There was no harm now in blushing happily at the love-light in Gerald's eyes, and her three companions were those she loved best in all the world. Her recent cares and heartaches seemed all to have been left behind in Cairo, and she could look forward to many weeks of keen enjoyment.

She was sorry, however, that she had misjudged Prince Kāra, and promised herself to implore his pardon immediately on her return to Cairo.

Gerald and Mrs. Everingham, while they did not disabuse Aneth's mind, were a trifle uneasy at the growing audacity of the dragoman's statements, and warned him to be more careful. After the girl had regained her health and self-possession, they would explain to her the truth of the matter and discredit Tadros freely; at present they were content to note her bright eyes and the roses creeping back to her cheeks.

Lord Roane had wisely decided not to ask questions. From what he overheard he understood that Kāra was now befriending Aneth instead of persecuting her, and this being the case, his own danger was reduced to a minimum. He could not understand the Egyptian's change of attitude in the least. If Kāra had intended merely to frighten him, he had succeeded admirably, and Roane told himself that the punishment he had already suffered through terror and despair was sufficient to expiate his long-forgotten sin against Hatatcha. But did Kāra think so? That was a question he could not answer, but he decided to defer all worries for the present at least.

Gerald Winston would have been less than human had he refrained from showing to Aneth, during these delightful days, how dearly he loved her and what happiness her companionship brought to him. The moonlit evenings on deck were sufficient to inspire the most bashful lover, and Gerald did not dare waste his golden opportunities. If he won Aneth at all, it must be on this trip, and under the spur of Mrs. Everingham's counsel to be bold, he soon put his fate to the test and marveled at his success. The girl had suffered too much to trifle with her lover's heart, and her consent was readily won. It was his intention that they be married while at Luxor or Aswan, there being English churches in both places and ample conveniences for a proper conduct of the ceremony. Roane was fond of Winston, and offered no objection to a plan which would ensure Aneth's happiness and which seemed to be defective only in its precipitancy.

The project pleased Aneth as much as it delighted her lover. In her days of misery, when she thought she had lost him forever, the full value of Gerald's love had been so impressed upon her that she clung to him now, realizing that he represented the full measure of her future happiness; still, she experienced an uneasy sensation that any unnecessary delay might prove dangerous. Her contract with Kāra, moreover, had taught her to face the possibility of a sudden marriage, and what was a hateful ordeal then would now become a crown of triumph.

"Whenever you like, Gerald," she said, "I will become your wife. I could never wish for other witnesses of my wedding than my dear grandfather and Mrs. Everingham; and happiness is such a precious thing and life so uncertain, that I have no desire to resist your proposal."

"Thank you, my dear one," he said, gravely.

"And I think I prefer Luxor to Aswan. It will be so romantic to be wed in the old Theban city, where the Egyptian princesses once made their home and where they lived and loved, will it not?"

"It shall be Luxor," he declared.

That week was one of never-to-be-forgotten delight. Even Tadros wore a perpetual smile, although this method of sweet communion between lovers was all new and amazing to him. He felt quite secure now for the first time since Kāra had asserted his power over the dragoman's destinies, and wondered—the thing being so easy—why he had so long hesitated to break with his arrogant and imperious master. As the dahabeah lazily breasted the languid current of the river, Tadros idly wondered what Kāra was doing now, and could not forbear a laugh at the thought of the Egyptian's anger and perplexity when he had discovered the flight of his proposed victims. Oh, well—Kāra had pitted his cunning against the dragoman's intelligence! It was little wonder he was discomfited.

On the afternoon of the seventh day they steamed slowly past Beni-Hassan, their moderate progress being due to the fact that the boat tied up from every sunset to the next sunrise. Beni-Hassan was a picturesque village as viewed from the river, where its filth and stench were imperceptible, and the groups of splendid palms lent a dignity to the place that a closer inspection would prove undeserved.

Aneth, seated happily by Gerald's side beneath the ample deck awning, admired the village greatly, and her lover promised to stop there on their return and give her an opportunity of visiting the famous tombs in the nearby hillside.

At twilight they anchored midway between Beni-Hassan and Antinoe, the boat lying motionless a few yards away from the east bank.

The evenings are delightful in this part of Egypt, and it was midnight before the passengers aboard the dahabeah sought their couches. Tadros, indeed, being wakeful, lay extended upon the stern deck of the steamer long after the others were asleep, engaged in thoughtfully gazing at the high bank and indulging in pleasant dreams of future prosperity when he had added Winston Bey's three thousand pounds to the snug savings he had already accumulated.

Presently a dark object appeared for an instant at the top of the bank and quickly vanished against the black surface below. Another succeeded it, and another.

Tadros scratched his head in perplexity. These dark objects seemed to have form, yet they were silent as the dead. He counted a dozen of them altogether, and while still pondering upon their appearance, being undecided as to whether they were ghosts or jackals, his quick ears caught a splash in the water beside the bank.

They were not jackals—that was certain; for those ravenous beasts never take to the water. Neither are ghosts supposed to bathe. From where he lay, the surface of the river was scarcely a foot distant, and, leaning well over the stern, Tadros managed to discover in the dim light several heads bobbing upon the water.

He ought to have given an immediate alarm, but terror rendered him irresolute, and before he had time to act, it was too late to arouse his fellow-passengers.

Clambering up the bow were half a score of naked Arabs, their knives held between their glistening teeth, their dark eyes roaming fiercely around.

Tadros' first impulse was to fight; but just as he was about to rise to his feet a man whom he knew bounded aft and sprang into the little cabin where the women lay asleep.

It was Kāra.

There was no indecision on the part of the dragoman after that. He slipped off the deck into the water with the dexterity of a seal sliding from a rock, and while a succession of terrified screams and angry shouts bombarded his ears, Tadros swam silently across the Nile toward the opposite shore.

The water was cold, and he shivered as he swam; yet the chill was from within rather than from without. There are no crocodiles in the Nile now; but in places there are serpents and sharklike fish that will bite a mouthful of flesh from a swimmer's leg. Tadros knew of this, but did not think of it just then. Reflected in his mind was Kāra's dark visage, grim and malignant, and with certain death facing him aboard the dahabeah, the dragoman's only impulse was to get as far away from the danger as possible.

The turmoil on the boat prevented his escape from being immediately noticed, and after a long swim, that nearly exhausted his strength, he reached the west shore and fell panting upon the hard earth.

Slowly regaining his breath, he strained his ears to catch any sound that might proceed from the dahabeah; but now an oppressive silence reigned on the opposite side of the river. The lights of the steamer gleamed faintly through the night, but the fate of those he had left on board was wrapped in mystery. Perhaps Kāra and his band of assassins would murder all except the girl; it was possible he would murder her as well. Anyway, the dragoman's connection with the enterprise had come to an abrupt ending.

A mile or so away was the little town of Roda, with its railway station. Tadros started to walk toward it, keeping well back from the edge of the bank so that he might not be discovered in case anyone pursued him.

His dejection and dismay at this sudden reversal of fortune were extreme. He had lost the last vestige of the jaunty bearing that usually distinguished him. With three thousand pounds already earned but irretrievably lost, and the knowledge that Kāra's merciless enmity would pursue him through life, the dragoman's condition was indeed deplorable.

He wondered what he should do now. Returning to Cairo was out of the question. He would go back to Fedah, his old home. Nephthys and her mother were there, and would hide him if Kāra appeared unexpectedly. Yes, Fedah was his only haven—at least until he had time to consider his future plans.

By and by he reached the station at Roda—the village named after the ancient island in the Nile opposite Cairo. A sleepy Arab porter was in charge of the place and eyed the dragoman's wet clothing with evident suspicion. When questioned, he announced that a train would go south at six o'clock in the morning.

Tadros slipped outside the station and found a convenient hiding-place against a neighboring house, where the shadows were so deep that he could not be observed. Here he laid down to rest and await the arrival of the train.

By daybreak his clothing had dried, but he observed with regret that his blue satin vest had been ruined by the river water and that his Syrian sash was disgracefully wrinkled. Next to life itself, he loved his splendid costumes, so that this dreary discovery did not tend to raise his dampened spirits.

When the train drew in he boarded it and found himself seated in a compartment opposite to Lord Consinor. They stared at each other for a moment, and then the viscount emitted a sound that seemed a queer combination of a growl and a laugh.

"It is Kāra's alter ego," he sneered, in English.

"Pardon me, my lord," said the dragoman, hastily, "the alliance is dissolved. I have even more reason than you to hate the prince."

"Indeed?" returned Consinor.

"He is a fiend emanating directly from your English hell," declared Tadros, earnestly. "I know of no other diabolical place where Kāra could have been bred. One thing is certain, however," he continued, with bitter emphasis, "I will have vengeance upon him before I die!"

There was no mistaking the venom of the man's rancorous assertion. Consinor smiled, and said:

"It would give me pleasure to share your revenge."

A sudden thought struck Tadros—a thought so tremendous in its scope and significance that he was himself astonished and stared blankly into the other's face. For a time he rode in silence, revolving the idea in his mind and examining its phases with extreme care. Then he inquired, cautiously:

"Where are you going, my lord?"

"To Assyut."

"I thought you had left Cairo long ago."

"So I did. I have been to Alexandria, but found nothing there to amuse me. I am now bound for Assyut, and from there I intend traveling to Aswan, and up to Wady Halfa."

"Are you in any hurry to reach there?"

"Not the slightest."

"Then leave the train with me at Kusiyeh. I have something to propose that will interest you."

Consinor studied him a moment.

"Does this program include our revenge?" he asked.

"Yes."

"Very well; I will do as you suggest."

"Good!" exclaimed Tadros. Then he leaned over and whispered: "Revenge and a fortune, my lord! Is it not worth while?"

XXII

The Dragoman's Inspiration

They left the train at the station opposite Fedah, and the dragoman secured a native to row them in his skiff across the river. Consinor asked no questions and appeared wholly indifferent as to their destination. Indeed, his life had been so aimless since his disgraceful flight from Cairo that he welcomed any diversion that might relieve its dull monotony.

When they arrived at Fedah, Tadros took him secretly to the hut of old Nefert, the bread-baker, which was directly across the street from the dwelling of Hatatcha, now owned by Kāra. The viscount was inclined to resent the filthiness of the hovel wherein he must hide, until the dragoman led him to the shade of the opposite archway and explained to him something of the project he had in mind.

Tadros began by relating the "royal one's" early history, emphasizing the fact that old Hatatcha had been able to support herself and Kāra without any labor whatever. Then he told of Hatatcha's death, and how he, Tadros, had discovered the valuable rolls of papyrus in Kāra's possession. From thence to the brilliant advent of the "prince" in Cairo was but a step, and the entire history permitted but one explanation— the fact that Kāra had knowledge of an ancient tomb containing great riches.

"Once," said the dragoman, "Kāra and I made a visit to Fedah; but I did not suspect his errand and so neglected to watch him, being at the time greatly occupied with a certain maiden. In the morning I found he had loaded his traveling cases with treasures—wonderful gems that have enabled him to live in princely fashion ever since."

"Where did he get them?" asked Consinor, eagerly.

"As I said, from some hidden tomb, the secret of which is known only to himself."

"Do you think he has carried all of the treasure away?"

"I have reason to believe that more remains than has ever been taken. Once, in an unguarded moment, Kāra told me that he could not spend it all in a thousand years."

"Do you suppose we can discover this tomb?"

"Yes, if we are clever. It is no use to hunt without a clew, but Kāra will furnish us the clew we need."

"In what way?" the viscount inquired.

"He is coming here presently."

Consinor frowned.

"I do not care to meet him," he said, hastily.

"Nor do I," rejoined Tadros, with a shudder; "but it will not be necessary for us to meet Kāra, who will not suspect we are in the village."

"What then?"

"He is coming to secure more treasure, his former supply being exhausted, as I have reason to know. He has promised his tradesmen money, and will not dare delay his visit to Fedah. Besides, he is not far from here at this very moment. By tomorrow, if he comes in Winston Bey's dahabeah, he will reach this place. If he decides to take a railway train, he may be here this evening."

"In that case, what do you propose to do?" demanded Consinor.

"Spy upon him; discover where the treasure is hidden, and when he is gone, help ourselves," was the confident reply.

The idea seemed quite feasible when further elaborated. They entered the room of Kāra's dwelling and examined the place carefully.

"This," explained the dragoman, "is doubtless his starting-point. From here he has either a secret passage into the mountain, or he steals away to the desert, where the entrance to the tomb is hidden underneath the shifting sands. We must be prepared to watch him in either event, and that is why I have proposed to you to assist me, rather than try to secure all the fortune myself. I am assured there is plenty for two, and to spare."

"Doubtless," replied the viscount, laconically. Already he saw visions of great wealth, which would enable him to return to London and rise superior to all the sneers and scandals that had been thrust upon him.

They discussed the matter long and earnestly, the few inhabitants of the village, stupid and inert, being entirely ignorant of their presence. It was finally decided that on Kāra's approach Consinor should conceal himself beneath the dried rushes of the old bed, Tadros so arranging his position that the viscount could observe every action of one moving within the room. Then the dragoman would himself lurk at the edge of the village to follow Kāra if he stole away into the desert.

As a matter of fact, Tadros was firm in his belief that the treasure was hidden within the mountain; but he had no intention of risking his own life when he could induce Consinor to become his catspaw. Discovery meant death—he knew that well enough. It was better not to take chances, and if the viscount succeeded in learning Kāra's secret it would mean the same to Tadros as learning it himself. He knew how to handle this outcast Englishman, and if the treasure proved as large as he suspected, he could afford to be generous, and would play fair with his accomplice. Otherwise—but that could be considered later.

Tadros did not desire to expose the stranger to the curious gaze of the villagers, but there was no harm in their knowing that the dragoman had come among his old friends once more; so he insisted that Consinor should stay concealed in Nefert's hovel, flying to a dark corner at the sound of every footstep, while he himself visited Sĕra and her daughter in furtherance of his sagacious plans.

XXIII

MOTHER AND DAUGHTER

As the dragoman approached Sĕra's hut he paused upon the threshold to observe the scene within, hesitating, as he remembered that it was because of his own reckless conduct that the Nile girl had been stripped of her beautiful gowns and jewels and sent home from Cairo scorned and repudiated.

Her humiliation and despair had haunted him ever since.

But now he found her seated meekly at the well-worn loom, casting the shuttle back and forth with the same mechanical lassitude she had exhibited of old. The discolored black dress, open at the breast and much patched and torn, was her sole garment. Even the blue beads were again about her neck.

But the eyes she turned toward Tadros were different, somehow. Their former velvety depths were veiled with a dull film, while the smoothness of her brow was marred by the wrinkles of a sullen frown.

After a moment, however, she seemed to recognize the dragoman, and rose from her place with a sudden eager look and flushed cheeks.

"You have come for me again?" she asked.

"No," answered Tadros, casting himself upon a settle. He felt abashed without knowing why he should entertain such a feeling—abashed and sorrowful, in spite of his habitual egotism and selfish disregard of others.

Nephthys leaned back and resumed her weaving. The film covered her eyes again. She paid no further attention to her mother's guest.

Sĕra, however, was voluble and indignant.

"That Kāra," she hissed, "is a viper—a crocodile—a low, infamous deceiver! He is worse than an Arab. Henf! If I had him here I would stamp him into the dust. Why did he spurn my beautiful daughter from his harem? Tell me, then!"

"Merely because Nephthys and I, being old friends, wished to converse at times of you and our acquaintances at Fedah. Why should we not gossip and smoke a cigarette together? Once I owned her myself."

"True. You were a fool to sell her."

"Still, you must not forget that Nephthys has had an experience," he resumed, more lightly. "For a time she was a queen, splendid and magnificent beyond compare in her robes of satin and her sparkling jewels. Ah, it is not every girl who enjoys such luxury, even for a brief season! Let her be content."

"Content!" screamed old Sĕra, shrilly; "it has ruined her. She is no longer happy in the old home, and when she speaks, which is but seldom, it is only to curse Kāra. Look at her! Is she now fat and beautiful as before? No. If the poor child lives long enough, she will die a skeleton!"

"Allah forbid!" exclaimed Tadros, hastily. "But if she expects to be taken back again, her case is hopeless. I sure Kāra will never relent or restore her to favor. He is a poor judge of a woman. But I," slapping his chest proudly, "I will take Nephthys to myself; and while I do not promise to robe her as gorgeously as did Kāra, she shall become fat again, and have her silks and ornaments the same as before."

"And the cigarettes?"

"Of course."

He drew a box of the coveted cigarettes from his pocket and tossed it toward her. Sĕra lighted one eagerly and gave the box to Nephthys. After staring at it blankly for a moment the girl seemed to understand. She took a cigarette and lighted it from the one her mother was smoking. A smile of childish enjoyment slowly spread over her face, and she left her loom and came and sat upon Tadros' knee.

"I expect Kāra in Fedah presently," remarked the dragoman. "But he must not know that I am here. We have had a falling-out. I quarreled with him, and he threatens me."

"Never fear," said Sĕra, calmly. "I can hide you in the cavity in the rear wall, which the royal one knows nothing of. There you will be safe until he goes away."

"Very good!" he replied.

"When will Kāra come?" asked the woman, "and why does he visit Fedah again?"

"I expect him tonight or tomorrow. Why he comes I do not know."

"Perhaps to pray beside Hatatcha's mummy."

"Where is that?" he asked, quickly.

"I cannot discover," she returned. "Often I have examined their dwelling, but no secret door can I find anywhere. The tomb must be in the hills—or perhaps in the desert. There is an oasis where the dwarf Sebbet lives. He was known to be one of Hatatcha's most devoted followers."

"True," said the dragoman, thoughtfully.

"The tomb must be in Sebbet's oasis. Once Kāra stole old Nikko's donkey and rode there."

"Was that the last time we came here?" questioned Tadros.

"No; it was when Hatatcha died."

"Then the tomb is not in the oasis. I am sure it is quite near Fedah. But listen, my Sĕra; if I agree to take Nephthys and provide for her, you must help me when Kāra comes."

"I have promised to hide you in the old wall," she replied. "Can I do more than that?"

"Yes. You must go at once to the hill and watch for the royal one's coming. Your eyes are sharp, even though you are old. He will come from the Nile—either across the river or from the north, on a boat that smokes and has no sails. As soon as you discover him you will hurry here to me, and that will give us time to prepare for Kāra. Will you do this for me?"

"May I have the box of cigarettes to take with me?"

"Yes."

"Then I will do your bidding."

She went away to the hill at once, leaving Tadros with Nephthys; but the girl had already forgotten his presence and was staring straight before her with lusterless eyes.

The dragoman sighed.

"It is very unfortunate," he murmured, examining her critically, "but it is doubtless true, nevertheless—she is getting thin."

XXIV

The Sheik Demurs

No one on board the dahabeah had entertained even a suspicion of danger. Winston Bey knew well the unreliable character of the natives of certain villages, but even he did not dream that the steamer would be molested or its passengers annoyed; therefore, the surprise was complete.

Mrs. Everingham, awakening with a start, heard the patter of many feet upon the deck and saw a man advancing into the cabin where she and Aneth had been sleeping.

Her first inspiration was to scream; but instead she reached beneath her pillow and drew out a small revolver, with which she fired two shots in rapid succession point blank at the intruder.

Neither bullet took effect, but they startled Kāra as much as her vigorous screams, in which Aneth now joined. He retreated hastily from the cabin, thus allowing Mrs. Everingham to close the door and secure it with a heavy bar provided for that purpose.

The after-cabin having been given up to the women, Winston and Lord Roane occupied a smaller cabin forward. Between the two were the kitchen and the engine-room. As the natives boarded the steamer near the bow, their first act was to drop into the forward cabin and seize the white men before they were fairly awake. Roane offered no resistance whatever, but Winston struggled so energetically that it took three of the men, headed by the gigantic sheik, to secure him. It required but a few moments to bind the prisoners securely hand and foot, and then they were left in their bunks under a guard of natives, who held their bare knives in their hands in readiness to prevent any possible escape.

The four Arabs of Winston's crew were easily overcome, and by the time that Kāra arrived forward they laid upon the deck carefully pinioned. There had been no bloodshed at all, and the steamer was now entirely in the control of Kāra and his mercenaries.

"All right," said the sheik, nodding his satisfaction as the Egyptian approached. "It was very easy, my prince. The two white men are below, and the boat is ours."

Kāra, by the dim light of a lantern, peered into the faces of his prisoners.

"Where is the dragoman?" he asked. "Did you kill him, as I commanded you to do?"

"We had not that pleasure," returned the sheik, "for he was not on board."

"Are you sure?"

"Very sure, my prince."

"He may be in hiding. Search every part of the steamer thoroughly except the cabin of the women."

The sheik shrugged his shoulders, but gave the command to his men. They examined every possible hiding-place without finding the dragoman.

Meanwhile Kāra squatted upon the deck, thinking earnestly of what his future action should be, while the silent sheik sat beside him with composed indifference. When the Arabs returned from their unsuccessful quest, the Egyptian said to his ally:

"Let your men watch the prisoners until morning. We can do nothing more at present."

So they stretched themselves upon the deck and rested until daybreak.

As soon as it was light enough to distinguish objects readily, Kāra arose and ordered Winston and Lord Roane brought upon deck. There they saw the Egyptian for the first time and understood why they had been attacked.

"I suspected that I owed this little diversion to you," said Winston, glaring angrily upon his enemy. "Perhaps you do not realize, Prince Kāra, that by this lawless act you have ruined yourself and your career."

"No," returned Kāra, smiling; "I do not realize that."

"These things are not tolerated in Egypt today," continued the Bey.

"Not if they are known," admitted Kāra.

"Do you think, sir, that I will remain silent?" demanded Winston, indignantly.

"Yes."

"And why?"

"Because I have no intention of permitting you to return to Cairo. Understand me, Winston Bey—I entertain no personal enmity toward you; but you saw fit to interfere with my purposes, and in doing so destroyed yourself. Having been lawless enough to capture your boat, an outrage only justified by my desire to obtain possession of the persons of Aneth Consinor and Lord Roane, I am compelled, in order to protect myself, to silence every person aboard who might cause me future annoyance. Therefore, it is necessary to kill you."

"You dare not!"

"You misjudge me," answered Kāra, coolly; "but I shall be glad to furnish you immediate proof of my sincerity." Turning to Antar, he said: "Comrade, oblige me by placing your knife in the heart of Winston Bey."

The sheik did not move.

"Well?" cried Kāra, impatiently.

"It is not in the compact," returned the imperturbable Arab.

"You are wrong," said the Egyptian, sharply. "It was fully understood you should obey my commands, especially as to killing those of my enemies whom I desired to silence."

"My brother will remember," returned the sheik, "that there was also another understanding—a little matter relating to certain jewels and piastres."

"You shall have them!"

"And you shall be obeyed—when I have them."

Winston smiled, and Kāra saw it and uttered a curse.

"Will you thwart me now, when it is too late for either of us to retreat with safety?" he asked Antar, angrily.

"By no means. I do not object to the killing, believe me, my brother; but my people are poor, and the money you have promised them will do much to ease their sufferings. Let me but see the gems and the piastres and all your desires shall be gratified."

Winston looked at the gigantic Arab closely. He seemed to remember the man, but could not place him, for Antar had not only trimmed his gray beard, but had dyed it a deep black. Still, all natives are crafty and covetous, and the words he had overheard gave him an idea.

"Listen, my sheik," he said in Arabic. "If it is money you wish, I will double Kāra's offer to you. It is but natural that a man will pay more for life than another will pay for revenge. State your price, and the sum shall be yours."

Antar turned toward the Egyptian, an expression of satisfaction upon his keen features.

"My brother will answer," he said.

"This is absurd," declared Kāra. "Winston Bey but trifles with you. His money is all in Cairo. When you go there to get it, he will throw you into prison, and your people will be destroyed and their houses torn down to satisfy the Government police."

"The noble sheik is no fool," observed Winston. "He will keep us in his power, closely guarded, until he has sent to Cairo and obtained the money. Also, I will promise not to betray him, and my word is as good as that of Prince Kāra."

"But why should he go to Cairo at all?" asked the Egyptian. "If he will but come with me to Fedah he shall have his price. Not all of Winston Bey's wealth can approach the magnificence of the treasure I will place in Antar's hands."

The eyes of the sheik sparkled.

"Good!" he exclaimed.

"You will be faithful to me?" asked Kāra.

"Why not?"

"There is much treasure at my command. Not a mere handful of gems shall be yours, but enough to make your tribe wealthy for all time to come."

"I believe that my brother speaks truth."

"Then," said Kāra, relieved, "I ask you to kill Winston Bey as a proof of your confidence in me. The others may live until we get to Fedah."

"Tah! What is the use of dividing the ceremony?" returned the sheik, with a gesture of indifference. "I like not this pig-sticking in sections. It means cleaning one's knife several times instead of once. Be patient, my brother. When we have arrived at Fedah and our friendship is further cemented by your royal generosity, then will I accomplish all the killing in a brief space and have done with it. Is it not so?"

Kāra hesitated, but saw clearly that the wily sheik would not trust him. Moreover, he feared that Winston's eager offers to outbid him, if persistently repeated, might prove effectual unless he carried out his own promises to the greedy Arab. He had not expected to pay Antar any great price for his services, and in the beginning intended that the "handful" of gems would be a very small one; but Antar had entrapped him cleverly, and he now realized he must expend an exorbitant sum to induce the old sheik to obey his orders.

After all, that did not matter. The entire treasure had been Hatatcha's before it descended to him, and a portion of it would be well expended in securing her vengeance. He alone knew that the hoard was practically inexhaustible, and he might even bury the big Arab in jewels and golden ornaments and still have left more than he could use in his own lifetime.

So he agreed, with assumed content, to Antar's proposition, and Abdallah, the engineer, was released from his bonds and instructed to start the dahabeah upon its voyage up the river. It would be thirty hours before they could hope to reach Fedah.

Roane and Winston were permitted to remain upon deck, but were tied to their chairs and carefully guarded. Breakfast was served, and Kāra accompanied the Arab who carried the tray to the cabin of the women. The Egyptian had not disturbed them since the night before, well knowing they had made themselves as secure as he could have done.

He rapped boldly upon the door and said:

"Let me in."

"Who is it?" asked Mrs. Everingham.

"Prince Kāra."

"By what right do you annoy us with your presence aboard this boat?" she continued.

"That I will explain when you permit me to see you," he answered.

For a few moments there was silence.

"Your breakfast is here, and the servant is waiting for you to open the door," continued Kāra.

Somewhat to his surprise the bar was removed, and Aneth threw the door wide open.

"One moment, please!" cried Mrs. Everingham, and as Kāra was about to enter he saw the lady standing in the middle of the cabin with her revolver pointed toward him.

"I was so startled last night that I missed you," she said, calmly; "but I am almost certain I can shoot straight this morning."

Kāra shrank back a little.

"Why do you fear me?" he asked.

"I don't," she answered. "It is you who fear, and with reason. But I do not trust you, because you have convinced me that you are a consummate scoundrel. If you have anything to say to me or to Miss Consinor, we are prepared to hear it; otherwise you had better go, for I am extremely nervous and my finger is upon the trigger."

"I have taken possession of this steamer," he announced. "All on board are now my prisoners."

"How dramatic!" she returned, with a laugh. "May I ask what you intend to do with us? Will you scuttle the ship, or raise the black flag and become a modern pirate of the Nile? Come, my buccaneer, confide to us your secret?"

"In due time, madam, you shall know all, and more, perhaps, than will please you," he answered, furious at her gibes. "One thing, however, is certain. Miss Consinor"—and here he cast an evil glare at the girl, who stood with white face in the background—"shall not escape me again. I intend to take her to Cairo and keep her secure in my villa. As for you, Mrs. Everingham, your life hangs by a thread. If I could depend upon your discretion and silence I might spare you; but you are clever enough to understand that I cannot afford to take chances of future accusations."

"My man," replied Mrs. Everingham, "your own miserable life is at this moment not worth a farthing's purchase. If you dare to molest this girl or me again, or even show your ugly face in this cabin, I swear to shoot you upon the spot. Here, Selim, bring in that tray. Place it on the table; that will do. Now, Prince Kāra, I will give you one minute to disappear."

That was too long; he was gone in an instant, his face contorted with rage as he cursed the woman who had so successfully defied him.

On deck he met the sheik.

"Tell the engineer to urge the boat forward," he said; "we must keep moving day and night until we reach Gebel Abu Fedah."

"Very good," responded the sheik. "I am even more impatient than you are, my brother. It is only the prisoners, who have been watching us sharpen our knives, that are in no hurry."

XXV

The Bronze Bolts

Old Sĕra kept watch faithfully that day and the next at her post of observation on the hill, finding solace through the tedium of the hours in an occasional cigarette from her precious box.

Soon after noon of the second day she hurried to Tadros.

"He is coming," she said.

The dragoman sprang up.

"From which direction?" he inquired.

"From down the river. He is in the steamboat, and in half an hour will be at the landing."

"Go back at once," commanded Tadros. "Wait until he lands, and then come to me immediately. I will be in Hatatcha's house."

Sĕra obeyed, and, to the dragoman's surprise, Nephthys followed her mother to the hill. The girl had roused herself when the old woman returned, and seemed to comprehend, from the eager conversation and the dragoman's orders, that Kāra was coming. She said nothing, however, but hastened after her mother and took a position beside her on the height commanding the river.

Tadros ran to the house of Hatatcha, where Consinor, having rebelled at the confinement in old Nefert's hovel, had that morning installed himself. It was as safe a refuge as the other, for none of the villagers ventured to enter the grim archway, and so long as the viscount escaped observation Tadros was content. There was little cheer in the gloomy room, however, and Consinor had begun to believe that he could scarcely be recompensed for the miserable hours of waiting by the promised reward when, to his infinite relief, his fellow-conspirator entered to announce that the long-anticipated time for action had arrived.

"There is not a moment to be lost," said Tadros. "Get under the rushes, quick!"

The viscount immediately burrowed beneath the dry rushes, and the dragoman placed him in such a position that his head was elevated slightly and rested against the stones of the wall, thus enabling him to observe every corner of the room through the loosely strewn covering.

Having safely concealed him, Tadros stood back and examined the rushes critically to satisfy himself that Kāra would have no suspicion that they had been recently disturbed. The arrangement was admirable. He could not see Consinor himself, even though he knew he was hidden there.

"Are you comfortable?" he asked.

"Not very."

"I mean, can you remain quietly in that position for an hour or more?"

"Yes," answered Consinor, through the rushes.

"Then I will go," announced Tadros. "Be very careful in your actions. Remember that a fortune for both of us hinges upon the events of the next hour, and we must make no mistake. I go to watch the street and the desert beyond. Farewell, and may fortune attend you!"

He left the house, dropping the ragged mat over the inner arch and then crossing to Nefert's hut.

Presently Sĕra came running toward him.

"He has landed and is coming this way," she reported.

"Very well. Go home."

"The cigarettes are all gone."

He tossed her another box, and soon she had disappeared within her own doorway. Nephthys was not with her, but Tadros had forgotten the girl just then.

He crept within Nefert's front room and hid himself in the shadows in such a way that he could see through the hole, which served as a window, the opposite archway of Hatatcha's dwelling.

Kāra entered the narrow street and looked cautiously around him. It pleased him that no curious native was in sight. The sheik and his band were in possession of the dahabeah and the prisoners, and were awaiting Kāra's return with impatience. Therefore, he must enter the secret tomb at once, without the cover of darkness to shield his movements; but the inhabitants of Fedah were dull and apathetic—they were not likely to spy upon him.

He glanced with pride at the ring he wore upon his finger. The talisman of Ahtka-Rā was indeed powerful, for it had enabled him to accomplish all that he desired, and was protecting him even now. Should he take this occasion to restore it to the tomb of his ancestor—that ancient one who had entreated that it be left with his mummy for all time, and had threatened with dire misfortune anyone who dared to remove it? Why should Kāra leave the precious Stone of Fortune in that mountainous dungeon? Why should he deprive himself of the powers it bestowed upon its possessor? It could not now benefit Ahtka-Rā, who was long since forgotten in the nether world; but it might be of service to Kāra in many ways. Yes; he would keep it, despite the pleading and curses of that dead one who so foolishly and selfishly wished it left with his mummy.

Perhaps some day, years hence, he would restore the stone to the sarcophagus from whence he had taken it; but not now. Again he looked at the strange jewel, which seemed of extraordinary brilliancy at that moment, shooting its tongues of flame in every direction. The curse? Henf! Why should he care for the curse of a mummy, when the greatest talisman of fortune in the world was his?

He slipped within the archway of his dwelling and drew the mat closely behind him. Tadros had marked his every movement, and now breathed a sigh of relief. For the present, at all events, the adventure was in Consinor's keeping rather than his own, and Consinor must suffer the risk of detection.

The dragoman settled himself upon an earthen bench and kept his eyes on the archway. Presently Nephthys came stealing into view, treading with the caution of a cat and crouching low beneath the stone arch. She did not attempt to draw aside the mat, but squatted upon the ground just outside the barrier. Tadros observed her curiously, and noticed that one of her hands was thrust within her bosom, as if clutching some weapon.

A dagger? Perhaps. Nephthys had been wronged, and might be excused for hating Kāra. Should the dragoman interfere to save him? To what end? Before the girl could strike, the royal one's secret would be in Consinor's possession, and then—why, Nephthys would save them any annoyance their discovery might entail. Clearly, it was not a case that merited interference.

Meantime Consinor had noted the entrance of Kāra, as well as the care with which the matting had been fastened to keep out prying eyes. It shut out most of the light, also; but that bothered the Egyptian more than it did the Englishman, whose eyes had now grown accustomed to the dimness.

Kāra had to feel his way along the wall to the secret crypt, but he knew the location of the place exactly, and soon found it. Consinor saw him take from the recess a slender bronze dagger with a queerly shaped blade, and an antique oil lamp. With these he approached the opposite wall of the room—that which was built against the mountain—and pushed vigorously against one of the stones.

It swung inward. The spy saw only blackness beyond; but his first consideration was to count the stones from the corner to the opening, and then to note that it was in the third tier or layer of masonry. By this time Kāra had crept through and closed the orifice.

Consinor was breathing heavily with excitement. The great discovery had been made with ease. All he need do was to wait until Kāra came out and left the village, and then he would be able to visit the secret tomb and its treasure-chamber himself.

But as the moments slowly passed—moments whose length was exaggerated into seeming hours—Consinor began to feel uneasy. He remembered that Tadros had impressed upon him the necessity of following Kāra wherever he went. The secret might not be all upon the surface.

Fearful that he had wasted precious time in delay, he threw aside the covering of rushes and approached the wall. It was scarcely necessary to count the stones. He had stared at them so long that he knew the exact spot which Kāra had touched.

Responsive to his push, the great stone again swung backward and he crept through as the other had done and found himself confronted with blackness.

The dragoman had foreseen such an event, and had thoughtfully provided his accomplice with a candle. Consinor lit it, and, leaving the stone entrance somewhat ajar, so that he might have no trouble in escaping if he were compelled to return in haste, he began a cautious exploration of the various passages that led into the mountain.

He lost sometime in pursuing false trails; but at length he came upon a burnt match, tossed carelessly aside when Kāra had lighted his lamp, and it lay within the entrance of a rough and forbidding-looking gallery between the rocks.

However, Consinor followed this trail, and after stumbling along blindly until it had nearly ended in a cul-de-sac, he came to a circular door in the cliff which stood wide open. Beyond was a passage carefully built by man into the very heart of the mountain.

The viscount paused to examine the door carefully. It had been most cleverly constructed, and fitted its opening accurately. Six huge bronze bolts, working upon springs, were ranged along its edge, and the single hinge was of enormous size and likewise composed of solid bronze.

But he could see no keyhole nor lever by means of which the door had been opened. The outer surface was an irregular rock, harmonizing with the side of the passage, but the edges and the inner surface were carefully dressed with chisels. An examination of the casing showed bronze sockets for the bolts securely embedded in the cliff, and he could understand that when the door was closed the bolts fastened themselves automatically. But how had it been opened? That was a mystery he could not penetrate; for Kāra, after unlocking the door, had inadvertently withdrawn the dagger from the secret orifice and carried it with him into the tomb. It was a foolhardy proceeding, for if by chance he dropped the dagger inside the passage, he would forever afterward be powerless to enter the tomb again, since it was the only key to the treasure-chamber in existence. Besides, the removal of the dagger from the orifice was useless; for, as Hatatcha had once explained to Kāra, the door could not be opened from the inside.

Consinor felt convinced that the Egyptian must have gone through this passage, so he cautiously entered the doorway. It was a long, straight way, slanting downward, and before he had proceeded far, the atmosphere became dense and stifling. Still, he decided that where Kāra had gone he also could go, and so persevered, holding the candle above his head and walking as swiftly as he dared.

Meantime the Egyptian had penetrated to the vast mummy chamber, where, because of his haste, he neglected to light any of the bronze lamps, depending alone upon the dim illumination which the flickering wick of his small lamp afforded. He passed the bodies of Hatatcha and Thi-Aten, with scarcely a glance in their direction, and hastened between the rows of mummy cases toward the upper end of the room. Here, majestically imposing, stood the great sarcophagus of Ahtka-Rā, its thousand jewels glittering wierdly in the fitful glare of the floating wick, as Kāra held the lamp close to its side to detect the secret spring in the malachite slab that opened the way to the treasure-chamber.

The stone slid back with a sound that seemed like a moan of protest, and the Egyptian gave a nervous start as, for the first time, a realization of his dread surroundings flashed upon him.

But he controlled himself and muttered: "Perhaps it is the ghost of my great ancestor, bewailing the loss of his talisman. If his spirit could creep back from the far nether world, it would doubtless demand of me the return of the Stone of Fortune. . . Not yet, Ahtka-Rā!" he called aloud, mockingly; "save your curse for a year longer, and it will not be required. Just now I have more need of the talisman than you have!"

With these words he crawled into the aperture and descended the steps to the room below. He had brought with him two canvas sacks, one of which he proceeded to fill with the poorest and least valuable of the ornaments that littered the place. Even then the tribute to Sheik Antar was far in excess of the value of his services, and Kāra groaned at the necessity of bribing the crafty Arab so heavily.

The other sack was to contain his own treasure, and that he might avoid frequent visits to this gloomy place, which he began to dread, he selected the rarest of the great gems and the richest golden jewelry for himself, tumbling all together into the receptacle until it was full to overflowing and could only be tied at the neck by shaking down the contents.

The two sacks were heavy when he picked them up to carry them away. He suspended the bronze lamp in front of him by attaching its chain to a button of his gray coat. Then, a burden under either arm, he ascended the stairs and stepped from the orifice into the chamber above.

As he did this, the weight of the treasure shifted, and he stumbled and fell heavily against the massive sarcophagus of Ahtka-Rā. The jar of the impact was enough to send the golden bust of Isis toppling from its place. It struck Kāra in the breast, upsetting the lamp and leaving him in total darkness. Then it rebounded and caught his hand, crushing it against the marble side of the tomb. The sharp pain caused by this made him cry out and cling, faint and ill, to the stones of the sarcophagus. There, motionless, he stood in the dark and listened while the bust fell into the opening at his feet, and slowly rolled, step by step, into the treasure-chamber beneath, finally adding itself with a hollow crash to the rich hoard the ages had accumulated therein.

Kāra shuddered. The awful incident, the blackness that enveloped him, the clamor of noise in that silent place and the quiet suspense succeeding it, all conspired to unnerve him and fill his heart with consternation. The sacks had fallen from his grasp. He raised his injured hand, felt it, and gave a sudden cry of terror. The ring containing his ancestor's precious Stone of Fortune had been broken by the blow and the talisman was gone.

Gone! Then the curse had fallen. It was upon him even now, and perhaps at his side stood the grim spirit of Ahtka-Rā, leering at him through the darkness and exulting in his discomfiture.

Trembling in every limb, the Egyptian fell upon his knees and began creeping here and there upon the clammy stones, his eyes staring into the gloom and his fingers clutching at every slight protuberance in the hope of finding again the wonderful stone that could alone protect him in his extremity. The curse was upon him, but he would resist its awful power. He *must* resist; for if he succumbed now, there would be no future escape from his fate. The stone—he must find the stone! Somewhere in that vast chamber of death it lay, slyly waiting for him to reclaim it.

The cold indifference that was an integral part of Kāra's nature had completely deserted him. The superstitious fear inherited by him from the centuries had gripped his heart securely and made him its bondman. He mumbled incoherently as, prone upon all fours, he shuffled hither and thither in his vain search. The words of warning contained in the tiny parchment, the solemn curse of his ancestor upon any who deprived him of the talisman of fortune, seemed alone to occupy a mind suddenly rendered witless and unruly by the calamity of the moment.

The darkness was oppressive. There was no sound since the golden bust had bumped its way into the treasure-chamber. The atmosphere, although fed and restored from some hidden conduit, seemed stagnant and full of the bituminous stench of the mummies. Kāra drew his quaking body about with an effort, feeling that the silence, the dead air and the blackness were conspiring to stifle him. He found the lamp presently, but the oil was spilled and the wick gone. It did not occur to him to strike a match.

"If the stone is here," he thought, "I shall see its flaming tongues even through the darkness. It cannot escape me. I must seek until I find it."

Twice he crept around the colossal sarcophagus of Ahtka-Rā, feeling his way cautiously and glaring into the darkness with distended eyeballs; and then came his reward. A streak of fire darted before his eyes and vanished. Another succeeded it. He paused and watched intently. A faint blue cloud appeared, whence the flames radiated. Sometimes they were crimson; then a sulphurous yellow; then pure white in color. But they always darted fiercely from the central cloud, which gradually took form and outlined the irregular oblong of the wonderful stone.

The radiance positively grew; the tongues of flame darted swifter and more brilliantly; they lighted the surrounding space and brought into relief the glistening end of Ahtka-Rā's tomb.

Kāra stared with an amazement akin to fear; for the talisman lay upon the floor just beneath the triple circlet of gold whence he had pried it with his dagger. It had not only escaped from its unlawful possessor, but had returned to where the ancient Egyptian had originally placed it; and now it mocked him with its magical brilliance.

He could have reached out a hand and seized it in his grasp; but so great was his horror of the curse of Ahtka-Rā that his impulse was rather to shrink from the demoniacal gem.

How wonderful was its brilliance! It lighted the sarcophagus and the wall beyond. It lighted the floor with a broad streak of yellow light. It lighted even Kāra himself, groveling before it on hands and knees. No ordinary gem could do this. It was sorcery, it was—

He uttered a scream that echoed horribly through the vault and sprang to his feet; for a glance over his shoulder had betrayed the secret of the strange illumination.

At the lower end of the room stood a man holding above his head a lighted candle. He was motionless, gazing curiously at the prone form of the Egyptian wallowing before a tomb encrusted with precious stones.

But now he returned Kāra's scream with a startled cry, and turned involuntarily as if to fly, when the other sprang up and advanced rapidly toward him.

Down past the rows of silent mummies sped the Egyptian, while Consinor awaited him in a stupor of indecision. Then, finally realizing his danger, he dashed the candle to the ground and ran up the passage as fast as he could go.

Kāra, although once more plunged into darkness by this action, knew the way much better than the Englishman, and did not for an instant hesitate to follow him. The curse of Ahtka-Rā was now forgotten—the talisman forgotten. Kāra realized that another had discovered his secret, and the safety of the treasure demanded that the intruder should not be permitted to leave the tomb alive.

Consinor, on his part, was slower to comprehend the situation; yet there was no doubt the Egyptian meant mischief, and the only means of escape lay up the long, narrow passage. As he fled he collided with the huge pillar that divided the library from the mummy chamber and rebounded against the wall of the gallery, falling heavily to the ground.

In an instant Kāra was upon him, his knee pressing the viscount's breast, his slender, talon-like fingers twined around his enemy's throat.

But when it came to wrestling, the Englishman was no mean antagonist. As the native released one hand to search in his bosom for the bronze dagger, Consinor suddenly grasped him around the middle and easily threw him over, reversing their positions, his body resting upon and weighing down that of the slighter Egyptian. Failing to find the knife, Kāra again gripped the other's throat with his powerful fingers.

There was but one thing to do in this desperate emergency. Consinor raised his enemy's head and dashed it against the stone floor. The Egyptian's grasp relaxed; he lost consciousness, and, tearing himself from the fatal embrace, the viscount rose slowly to his feet, his brain reeling, his breath gradually returning to him in short gasps.

For a few moments he leaned against the wall for support; then, rousing himself to action, he tottered slowly along the passage, feeling his way by keeping one hand against the wall of rock.

He had not proceeded far, however, when a rustling sound warned him that Kāra had returned to life. His ears, rendered sensitive by his fearful plight, told him that his enemy had arisen, and he heard the fall of footsteps pursuing him.

But Consinor was already retreating as rapidly as possible, impelled to swiftness by the spur of fear. Proceeding through the intense darkness, at times he struck the sides of the rocky gallery with a force that nearly knocked him off his feet; but in the main it was a smooth and straight way, and the Egyptian did not seem to gain perceptibly upon him, being evidently as dazed by the blow upon his head as was the Englishman by the throttling he had endured.

And so they pressed on, panting along through the stifling atmosphere, until suddenly Consinor ran full against the rocky end of the passage and fell half stunned upon the floor. He heard the pattering of Kāra's footsteps, the sound indicating that the Egyptian was gradually drawing nearer, and, dazed as he was, realized that sudden death menaced him. With a final effort he sprang to his feet, tumbled through the circular opening, and slammed the door into place with all his remaining strength.

He heard the sharp click of the bolts as they shot into their sockets, and the muffled cry of terror from the imprisoned Kāra.

Thoroughly appalled at what he had done, he again arose to his feet and moved rapidly along toward the entrance to the outer corridor.

For a certain distance the floor of this natural passage was as smooth as that of the artificial one, and before he came to the rougher portion,

Consinor saw a dim light ahead that came from the opening in the wall of the room.

All semblance of composure had now deserted him. His cowardice fully manifested itself at his first discovery, and he was not sure, even now that the bronze bolts shut in his enemy, that he was safe from pursuit. With Kāra's despairing cry still ringing in his ears, he reached the wall, passed through the opening, drew the stone into place behind him as a further precaution, and then sped in a panic across the room.

Nephthys heard him coming and thought it was Kāra. As he tore down the matting and dashed through the arch, the girl rose to her feet and viciously thrust out her hand.

Consinor fell with a moan at her feet, drenching the hard ground with a stream of blood. By the time Tadros had rushed to his assistance he was dead.

The dragoman, on ascertaining that the victim was his accomplice, was frantic with despair. He rushed into the dwelling and gazed around him anxiously. The room appeared to his eyes just as it had a hundred times before. Kāra was nowhere to be seen, and the secret that Tadros had plotted so artfully to discover was lost to him forever.

"Confound you, Nephthys!" he cried, returning to the archway, "you've killed the wrong man and eternally ruined my fortunes!"

But the girl had disappeared. In her mother's hut she had quietly seated herself at the loom and resumed her work at the shuttle.

XXVI

The Dragoman Wins

A ntar, the sheik, waited for Kāra until his patience was exhausted; then he left the dahabeah and came up through the sands to Fedah to discover, if possible, what had delayed the prince from returning with his promised reward. To Antar this cluster of hovels seemed mean and unattractive when compared with his own village, and these hills were not likely places for treasure tombs. He knew that the French and Italian excavators had been all over them, and found only some crocodile mummy pits.

The sheik grew suddenly suspicious. Kāra's promises were too extravagant to be genuine; doubtless he had deceived Antar from the first, and sought to obtain his services without payment. It was true that Kāra was reputed in Cairo to be wealthy, but he might easily have squandered his inheritance long ago. One thing Antar was certain of—the Egyptian prince must produce his treasure at once or the sheik, thinking he was duped, would undertake to exact a bit of vengeance on his own account.

Thus musing, he turned the corner of the hill and came full upon Tadros, who was expecting him. The dragoman's thumbs were thrust into the pockets of his gorgeous silver and blue vest. He stood with his feet spread well apart, in an attitude of dejection; his countenance was sorrowful and discontented.

"Ah," growled the sheik, "this is the man Kāra requested me to kill!"

"I do not doubt it," returned Tadros, meekly. "It is so much easier to kill one than to pay him the wages he has earned."

"Does he owe you money?" demanded Antar, sharply.

"Yes; and now I shall never get it."

"Why not?"

"Have you not heard? Prince Kāra came to this village a few hours ago and was met by a captain of police, who wants him in Cairo for more than a dozen crimes."

"What! Have you brought the police upon us?" exclaimed Antar, angrily.

"I? How absurd! I came here to get my money; but they have taken Kāra south to meet a detachment of soldiers who are coming from

Assyut. Presently they will return here in force to rescue Winston Bey, who is in some trouble through Kāra's actions."

"You are lying to me," declared the sheik. "It is you who have set the officers upon us. You are a traitor!"

Tadros appeared distressed.

"You have known me long, my sheik," said he, "and have always found me an honest man. Never have I mixed with the police in anyway. But do you imagine the Government will neglect to watch over Winston Bey and protect him from his enemies? Ask the captain when he returns with the soldiers and Kāra. He will be here very soon now, and he will tell you that Tadros the dragoman had nothing to do with his coming here."

The sheik glanced around nervously.

"You say he will be here soon?"

"At any moment. Something has gone wrong with Winston Bey's dahabeah, it seems, and the soldiers are to put things right."

Antar fell into the trap. In common with most natives, he greatly feared the mounted police, and had no inclination to face a company of them. Quickly he ran to the end of the hill overlooking the river, and blew a shrill blast between his fingers as a signal to his comrades.

Instantly his men swarmed from the distant boat and sped over the sands toward him. The sheik met them and the whole band turned toward the north, quickly disappearing among the rugged crags of the mountains.

Tadros, convulsed with laughter at his easy victory, watched until the last Arab was out of sight. Then he walked down to the dahabeah, where, in the gathering twilight, he cut the bonds of the prisoners, assuring Winston Bey and his party, with many bombastic words, that he had vanquished their enemies and they owed their lives to his shrewdness and valor.

"You are free as the air," said he. "Fear nothing hereafter, for I will now remain with you."

"Where is Kāra?" asked Winston.

Tadros did not know; but he suspected that Consinor, before returning from the interior of the treasure-chamber, had murdered the Egyptian, whose mysterious disappearance could in no other way be explained. Not wishing to mention the viscount's name, whose murder might involve both Nephthys and himself in trouble, he stuck to his original lie.

"Kāra is fleeing in one direction and the Arabs in another," he said, pompously. "I am too modest to relate how I have accomplished this remarkable feat; but you must admit I have been wonderfully clever and successful, and by remaining faithful to your interests, have saved you from a terrible fate."

Winston did not answer, for he was just then engaged in holding Aneth in a close embrace, while Mrs. Everingham looked upon the happy pair with moist eyes and smiling lips.

But old Lord Roane felt that their rescuer merited more tangible acknowledgment of his services.

"You are a brave man, Tadros," he said.

"I am, indeed, sir," agreed the dragoman, earnestly.

"When we return to Cairo I will see that you are properly rewarded."

Tadros smiled with pleasure.

"Thank you, my lord," said he; "it is no more than I deserve."

"Just now," continued his lordship, "we are bound for Luxor to celebrate a wedding."

"With Tadros for dragoman," remarked the Egyptian, calmly lighting a cigarette, "all things are possible."

A Note About the Author

L. Frank Baum (1856–1919) was an American author of children's literature and pioneer of fantasy fiction. He demonstrated an active imagination and a skill for writing from a young age, and was encouraged by his father who bought him the printing press with which he began to publish several journals. Although he had a lifelong passion for theater, Baum found success with his novel *The Wonderful Wizard of Oz* (1900), a self-described "modernized fairy tale" that led to thirteen sequels, inspired several stage and radio adaptations, and eventually, in 1939, was immortalized in the classic film starring Judy Garland.

A Note from the Publisher

Spanning many genres, from non-fiction essays to literature classics to children's books and lyric poetry, Mint Edition books showcase the master works of our time in a modern new package. The text is freshly typeset, is clean and easy to read, and features a new note about the author in each volume. Many books also include exclusive new introductory material. Every book boasts a striking new cover, which makes it as appropriate for collecting as it is for gift giving. Mint Edition books are only printed when a reader orders them, so natural resources are not wasted. We're proud that our books are never manufactured in excess and exist only in the exact quantity they need to be read and enjoyed.

bookfinity™

Discover more of your favorite classics with Bookfinity™.

- Track your reading with custom book lists.
- Get great book recommendations for your personalized Reader Type.
- Add reviews for your favorite books.
- AND MUCH MORE!

Visit **bookfinity.com** and take the fun Reader Type quiz to get started.

Enjoy our classic and modern companion pairings!

Classic & Modern

9 781513 211756